Not Broken
True Destiny Book 5
By Dana Marie Bell

Dana Marie Bell Books
www.danamariebell.com

This book is a work of fiction. The names, characters, places, and incidents are products of the writer's imagination or have been used fictitiously and are not to be construed as real. Any resemblance to persons, living or dead, actual events, locale or organizations is entirely coincidental.

Dana Marie Bell
PO Box 39
Bear, DE 19701

Not Broken
Copyright © 2014 by Dana Marie Bell
ISBN: 978-1985378506
Edited by Tera Kleinfelter
Cover by Angela Waters

All Rights Are Reserved. No part of this book may be used or reproduced in any manner whatsoever without written permission, except in the case of brief quotations embodied in critical articles and reviews.
First Edition electronic publication by Samhain Publishing, Ltd.: December 2014
Second Edition electronic publication by Dana Marie Bell: March 2017
First Edition print publication by Dana Marie Bell: February 2018

About the Author

Dana Marie Bell lives with her husband Dusty, their two maniacal children, an evil ice-cream stealing cat and a dog who thinks barking should become the next Olympic event. You can learn more about Dana and her addiction to series at www.danamariebell.com.

Dedication

For Mom, who couldn't understand why I'd rather sit in a locked room reading mythology than outside riding a bike, but got me a library card anyway. Have I mentioned I love libraries?

To Dad, who let me "work" in his barber shop when he first opened up. (Mostly, "work" involved me sitting in a quiet corner reading and occasionally sweeping up hair to earn my allowance. Meh, it's a living.)

And to Dusty, who gets to reap the benefits of all that research into mythology whenever he's playing video games involving it. Go me. (Does this make me the Nerd Whisperer?)

Prologue

Magni grimaced as Thor turned away from his wife Sif, ignoring her once more in favor of some serving wench who had just thrust her breasts in his face. The pain on Sif's face made Magni want to snarl in rage. It was a well-known fact that Thor could not keep his manhood in his trousers. One only had to look at his bastard sons, Magni and Modi, to see that.

How could his father dishonor his wife in such a way? If Sif belonged to Magni he would never cheat on her, never bring another to his bed. He would adore her to the end of his days. He would ignore his cravings for harder flesh and cleave unto her until Ragnarrok.

But Sif only saw Thor, worshipping the ground her husband walked on, and Magni was forced to treat her as his father's wife rather than the woman who Magni desperately wished graced his bed and his life.

"Easy, brother." Modi's hand landed on his shoulder, his twin's presence calming the rage within him, as it always did. "Calm yourself."

Magni's fists clenched as his father patted the bottom of the serving wench, his expression filled with lust. A lust that should rightfully belong to his wife.

"Perhaps this will help open her eyes to what Father truly is," Modi whispered in his ear, his words making no sense. Modi had been warning Magni not to lust after their stepmother for decades, to no avail. So why was he suddenly offering Magni his full support?

There was only one answer for the odd way his brother was acting. "Stop, Loki."

The man laughed, his face morphing into that of the Trickster God. Loki's face was filled with mischief, tiny flames dancing within his dark eyes. His reddish-brown hair was pulled back into a tail, and his leather armor was pristine. "What?" He leaned close, his breath tickling Magni's ear and sending an unwanted shiver down his spine. "You know you want her."

"What I want is irrelevant." He pushed Loki away, careful of his greater strength. As much as the Trickster was annoying, he was rarely vicious with Magni. "Only she matters."

For an instant sympathy shone through the roguish grin before it was quickly wiped away. "To want without surcease, to need without end, to desire with no outlet. That is true torture."

"I have outlets." Ones he would not share, not even with Modi, let alone Loki. The Trickster would use the knowledge against him, of that Magni had no doubts. He had done so before, driving a wedge between the gods and goddesses as he revealed their infidelities to one another.

Magni would not hand him the spear needed to pierce his heart and humiliate him. No. Better to keep his *outlet* secret than face his family.

Loud laughter drew his attention once more to Odin's table. Thor was laughing at something Odin had said, the Old Man looking pleased with his son. It was obvious that Thor was his favorite child, much to Frigg's disgust. A bastard himself, Thor was the mightiest warrior to walk Asgard. Baldur, for all his beauty, could not hold a candle to his half-brother when it came to battle.

Magni and Modi had no place at that table with their father and grandfather. The bastard sons of Thor, they'd been born of a jotun and as such were considered a shameful addition to Odin's family tree. Yet the leader of the gods allowed Loki, a fire giant, to sit where he willed, though Loki rarely chose the high table where Odin held court. No, the Trickster usually chose to sit among the so-called lesser gods, inciting mayhem among them and whispering sedition into their ears.

"Perhaps she longs for a real man between her thighs." Loki leaned closer, his hair brushing Magni's cheek as he whispered Magni's most shameful secret. "Or perhaps you do."

Magni stood, his anger burning along with his humiliation. "Shut your foul mouth, Trickster."

Loki laughed, leaning back in his chair. "Too close to the truth, Magni?" Magni snarled, but Loki merely grinned. "Have no fear, that particular secret is safe with me." Loki winked. "My heart may be shriveled and black, but I still have one."

Magni sucked in a breath as the Trickster's gaze darted toward Baldur. The longing glance was as familiar as the hilt of his sword.

Loki loved the other man as Magni loved Sif, and with just as much chance of gaining his desire as Magni had.

For a moment Magni felt sympathy for the other god. He knew intimately what it was to desire someone who was forever out of reach. "And yours with me."

Loki shot him a wide-eyed look before his expression changed, becoming the lazy, self-indulgent one Magni was used to seeing. "A bargain, then. Done and done, my angry friend."

That vow settled over Magni like a hot summer day. Loki would keep his secret, for while the Trickster loved to play with the gods, he had a strange sense of honor. Once given, his word was inviolate.

Magni nodded sharply, acknowledging the vow, before saying his good-byes to his brother Modi and striding from the dining hall. Watching Sif suffer had taken what little appetite he had for food.

Now he was off to indulge a completely different appetite.

Magni opened the door to his chambers and smiled. The slicked-up young man he'd chosen for the evening shot him a sultry glance over his shoulder, the round globes of his perfect ass shining with oil. "My lord. I've been waiting for you."

Magni shut the door, ready to sate his other hunger.

Chapter One

Slade Saeter watched his mate, Magnus Tate, size up the frail woman before them, and had to hide his satisfied smile against Magnus's chest. He'd waited centuries for this moment.

From the look on Magnus's face, Slade was going to have more than he'd ever dreamed was possible.

It still shocked him that the stunning redhead with the glittering green eyes and broad shoulders was his. Slade had given up hope of ever being able to claim Magni, now known as Magnus. Slade had been hiding in his horse form for so long, trying to avoid detection from Odin, that the dream of claiming Magni had become just that, a wish that could never be fulfilled. And the dream of Sif, of her long golden hair and flashing blue eyes, had been so far beyond his reach as to be ridiculous.

To claim either of them would have meant an end to all their lives. Odin would have gone into a fury at being deceived. He would have destroyed everything Slade yearned for before he could have more than a taste of it. It was something Slade still feared, still had nightmares about that woke him shaking and sweating in the dark. So he'd waited, and he'd watched, and he'd used every ounce of his strength to silently protect the people he cared for most in the world. He'd taken everything Odin could throw at him and remained the loyal beast as he waited for the signs of Ragnarrok. He'd only acted when he'd been certain it was time, but he'd been terrified that he'd be caught, unable to get away, forced to share Odin's fate in the final hour.

He'd done it anyway.

It was turning out to have been worth all the pain Odin had inflicted on him.

As Sleipnir he'd been thought of as nothing more than an animal, the favored steed of the leader of the gods. He'd died a little each day until he'd thought nothing was left. He'd watched Magnus take lovers one after another, and had his heart broken right along with Sif's when Thor cheated on her. Both of them deserved so much more than what they'd gotten, and he'd desperately wished to be the one to take them and make them his own. He would cherish every ounce of affection they chose to give him. And he would fight to the death to protect them.

Once he'd revealed that he was just like his siblings Hel, Jörmungandr and Fenris, he'd finally been able to begin claiming one of his mates, Magnus. He'd even chosen a mortal name that honored his father, Logan: Slade Saeter.

His father had come to rescue him when Slade needed him most, proving to Slade that he *was* cared for, even if he hadn't been aware of it. Logan, once known as Loki, was beyond thrilled that Sleipnir was in his home. He hovered over Slade, making sure he was warm enough and had anything he could possibly want. The only people who got that much attention from his father were Logan's mates, Jordan and Kir.

It hadn't surprised Slade to find that his father had finally mated Kir, once known as the god Baldur, and taken off with him. Loki had always longed for the younger, pretty god. Sleipnir could smell his desire every time Baldur was in the same room with him, but not even Loki had the balls to try and get Baldur to cheat on his wife, Nanna. Baldur had adored his deceased spouse, and only the worst of circumstances had separated them.

But when Odin tried to kill Baldur, things had changed dramatically. Loki had taken Baldur's place, tricking the others into believing Baldur was dead. Instead, Baldur had freed Loki from the chains he'd been placed in when Loki was blamed for Baldur's death. The two had run, Loki proving his devotion to Baldur over the years until Baldur could no longer live without the fiery jotun. When Jordan had joined them, their lives were complete.

Slade wanted that. He wanted the same thing his father had with his two mates. Logan, Kir and Jordan were inseparable, and utterly devoted to one another. Jordan carried the fruit of their love, their children growing inside her. One was of Logan, meaning Slade would soon have a tiny brother or sister to love. The other was of Kir, the new king of the gods, the man Logan had nearly given his life for. Slade would love that child like a sibling as well, for as far as he was concerned it would be.

He wanted to watch his woman swell with their children, children with Magnus's fiery red hair and Slade's dark eyes. Or maybe their mate's golden locks and Magni's pretty green eyes.

Magnus stood with him, holding him in his arms with all the care and tenderness Slade could ever want or desire. And still it was not enough. He wanted it all. He wanted Sif, who'd chosen the mortal name Sylvia Grimm. She stood before them with trembling lips and hope in her gaze. They needed their third, the one who would make them complete. And Slade needed his father to accept that she'd now be a part of their lives, whether Logan liked it or not. Slade hoped that Magnus would be open to what he was going to suggest.

"What are you doing here?"

Or maybe not. Magnus sounded far sterner than he ever did when speaking with Slade.

Sylvia bit her lip, looking so uncertain, so fragile.

Slade whimpered, hiding his face against Magnus's chest as the pain of what Odin had done to all of them slashed through him. He was still hurting, still healing from the horrors Odin had inflicted on him. Only Magnus knew the true extent of what Odin had done to him, over and over, before Magnus had rescued him. He'd been there in the night, holding Slade, weeping along with him when the terror became too much for Slade to bear. Odin had murdered Thor, taken the god from his children. And poor Sylvia had been under his thumb longer than any of them, forced to watch as the Aesir crumbled under the weight of prophecy.

He wanted his mates to stand by his side, to help one another rather than fight each other. He just wasn't certain how to accomplish that.

"I..." Sylvia's voice was uncertain.

Slade felt sorry for her. She'd been constantly pushed aside, by Thor, by Odin, and now by Frederica, who used her whenever it was convenient and forgot her otherwise. Sylvia had once been a formidable goddess. To see her reduced to a woman with a quivering lip, lost and begging, broke his heart.

"You?" Kir and Logan stepped in front of Magnus, more than likely preparing to protect Slade. What they thought Sylvia would do to him, Slade didn't know. She'd been fierce and brave when she'd been with Thor, but even she wouldn't dream of challenging Baldur, or Kir as he was now known. With the God of Spring holding the Godspear, *Gungnir*, he should now be the undisputed king of the gods. It was the symbol of his office, showing that the mantle had officially passed from Odin to his son. Odin had shit purple kittens when he'd lost *Gungnir* to Baldur. It was one of the happiest days of Slade's life.

"I want to join with you." Sif...No, *Sylvia's* tone was firm. Slade was still getting used to the mortal names of the Aesir. He'd been in Valhalla for so long he'd only heard the mortal names in passing.

Slade risked a peek at Sylvia. She had squared her shoulders, her expression determined, ready to do battle and win her verbal war. Sylvia needed them, and Slade and Magnus needed her. He just had to convince everyone to see things his way. Everything was within his grasp, and while he loved his father all the more for trying to save him, this time Slade didn't want to be saved.

Logan edged a little in front of Kir. "How do we know you're not a spy? Frigg could have sent you here to sabotage us."

Sylvia shook her head, her expression sad. "I wanted to join you that day at Fred's house, when you found *Mjolnir*, but I wasn't certain I would be welcome." She glanced at Logan, pushing her golden hair behind her ear. "Sydney wants to come too."

He could only imagine Logan's expression. His ex-wife would be an uncomfortable addition to their little family, especially since she still yearned for Logan with all her immortal heart. Whereas Sylvia had accepted Thor's desire to be with the woman he loved, Sydney had never seemed to give up hope that one day Logan would return to her.

Logan shook his head. "Jordan won't—"

Sylvia held up her hands in a pleading gesture that nearly broke Slade's heart. "Please? She's over you, I swear it. She wants the best for you and you have that. She...*we* just want to be free of Frigg."

Slade understood. Neither was strong enough to withstand a woman who'd once been the queen of the gods. "But you can't, not without someone strong to protect you." He tried to hide his wince. It still hurt to talk sometimes, and he doubted his voice would ever lose the painful rasp. It was Odin's last gift to him, one he wished he could give back in spades.

Magnus looked stunned at Slade's words. "You think we should allow it."

Slade looked up at him and went on tiptoe to whisper in his ear. "She's ours."

Magnus reared back and stared down at him with a mixture of hope, fear and longing on his face. "Are you sure?"

"As sure as I am that you're mine." Slade patted Magnus's chest. *Oh, muscles. Yum.* "She needs us."

Magnus studied him for a moment, ecstatic hope flaring across his face, before nodding. "All right."

"All right? Are you insane?" Logan scowled at Magnus. "You really want her around my injured son?"

Kir watched Sylvia with something approaching disapproval. "You'll need to prove yourself before we'll allow you to join us. Either of you."

Sylvia shivered, but stood her ground. She straightened her slim shoulders, the fragility now more like dignity and pride. "I can do that."

Kir studied her for a few moments, then glanced over at Logan. When Logan grimaced, Kir smiled and turned back toward Sylvia.

Slade held his breath. Whatever Kir said now would determine whether or not Slade got his wish.

"Find out what Frederica is up to. I don't trust her, she's been far too quiet recently."

Sylvia paled, but nodded. "Sydney will be able to come too?"

Kir nodded. "You have my word."

"Done." The ring of magic was in Sylvia's voice. She'd agreed to the bargain, but at what price?

"Wait." Slade held out his hand, well aware of how badly it shook. "Come here."

Sylvia took a tentative step forward.

Slade pulled out some of his white hair, barely feeling the sting. After everything he'd been through a few hairs being pulled out meant nothing to him. He braided them together into a bracelet. "Wear this. If you get into trouble you can't get out of I'll know and come for you."

Magnus growled, his arms tightening protectively around Slade. "*We'll* come for you."

Slade hid his smile again on Magnus's broad chest. The man said some of the best things ever. No one, not Kir, not even Logan, made him feel as safe as Magnus did.

Slade needed that sense of safety, of belonging, to extend to Sylvia as well. If he had his way their mate would join them sooner rather than later, and they'd be able to consummate their mating once and for all.

No one could take this joy away from him now. Not Odin, not Frigg, not the Fates themselves. Slade knew how to bide his time, how to wait in the shadows, unseen and unremarked. He'd keep watch over Sylvia without any of them ever knowing. He could slip away before any of them even realized it, just as he had when he'd called to warn them that Odin was coming for them. He'd learned long ago how to keep Odin's wards from detecting him when he didn't wish it. As strong as Logan's wards were, Slade could slide through them with ease, and would do so should the need arise.

Sylvia would be safe as he'd never been. Slade would see to it or die trying.

***

This wasn't the way things were supposed to happen. Sylvia had prayed that they'd let her in, that they'd see how desperately she wanted to get away from Frederica and her desire to destroy Logan Saeter and any who chose to side with him. Instead, Kir and Logan had sent her right back into the mouth of the dragon.

Not even chocolate chocolate-chip ice cream could fix this level of depression.

"Well?" Sigyn, who'd taken the mortal name Sydney Saeter, opened the door of their shared apartment with a hopeful expression.

Sylvia shook her head. "They want us to spy on Frigg and find out what she's up to or they won't let us join them."

Sydney's shoulders slumped. "Porcupine balls. That won't be easy."

Sylvia took Sydney's hand and led her into the apartment, closing the door behind her. "We can do this, Syd. If we find out what Frederica is up to, they'll accept us."

"Sure. Easy peasy." Sydney groaned as she dropped ungracefully into her office chair. "Why don't they ask for the moon? It would be easier."

"I know, right?" Sylvia settled on the sofa, the bright blue cheering her as it always did. "Logan looked good, by the way."

"Good." Sydney smiled softly. "After everything he's been through he deserves some happiness."

"He's found it." Sylvia was aware of Sydney's lingering feelings for Logan, but there was little she could do about it. Logan had fallen in love with Kir long before he'd been tied to that mountain. Worse, he'd never loved Sydney. He'd married her in order to cement his position in the Aesir, and because it was expected of him.

Sydney had adored him from day one and had believed in him when no one else did. In return he'd left her behind, running with Kir and hiding from all of them for centuries.

It was the best thing he ever did for Sydney Saeter, and he probably knew that. He was far more intuitive than Frigg gave him credit for.

Sydney had been forced to stand up for herself, to face the accusations that she was the one who'd freed him. But Odin had used his powers on her, the truth spilling forth from her like the poison of the snake that had tortured Loki. She'd gone to empty the bowl of venom, as she did whenever it filled. As she'd poured it away, she'd realized Loki wasn't crying out as he normally did. Without the bowl, the venom would land on his skin, burning him. He always cried out when she was forced to leave him in order to empty the bowl.

When she returned, he was free of his shackles, gone without a trace. And she had no idea who had done it.

Odin's use of the apples of Idunn had saved Sydney from being killed by Vali, the Avenger. She was innocent, by Odin's decree, but now she was terrified of Val Grimm. Whenever the large man entered the room Sydney would go still and quiet, afraid he would turn on her at any moment. He'd terrified her then, and still did. That he'd joined willingly with Kir and Logan only meant he was up to something, and Sydney was determined to find out what. She would not allow her ex-husband's happiness to be ruined by a spy of Odin's.

Too bad neither she nor Sydney had been aware of Odin's murderous intentions until it was far too late to do anything about it. Perhaps they could have helped more, done more. Things might have turned out far differently. Maybe Sydney wouldn't have this overwhelming fear of Val, because Sylvia had seen the way Sydney eyed Vali when she thought no one was looking.

Her friend had the hots for the Avenger, but was terrified of him at the same time. She denied it by believing Vali to be an enemy, one she had to harden her heart against.

It was a conundrum only time and proximity would cure. Sylvia planned on getting Sydney both.

Odin's use of the apples had kept them all happy little lambs, doing his bidding without a qualm. The only one who hadn't been affected was Logan, who hadn't deserved half the ire he'd received over the years. Without the influence of the apples, the Aesir and Vanir were finally able to see Odin and his machinations for what they were: a desperate attempt to stave off Ragnarrok.

It was too late. Ragnarrok was coming and nothing could stop it. Already the prophecies were coming true in ways none of them could have predicted. Thor was dead by the serpent's hand, but instead of Jörmungandr—the world serpent—being the murderer, it had been Odin—the betrayer—the *true* serpent in their midst. Loki had been killed by the Guardian of the Bifrost Bridge, Heimdall, but instead of it being the real Loki it had been Rina Sutherland, Odin's mistress, wearing Loki's face. She'd tried to trick the Guardian, but he hadn't been fooled. He'd seen right through the facade to the heart of the jotun beneath, and had killed her. She'd returned to her original form upon death, but she'd died wearing Loki's face.

It had all of them, Frederica included, looking at the prophecy with new eyes. What else had they gotten wrong all those years ago? If Fenrisúlfr wasn't meant to kill Odin, then who was the wolf destined to take his life? Or could Fenris only kill him at a specific place and time, when Odin would be vulnerable? Was there something Fenris would have to obtain in order to gain the power to kill him? And if so, would Vali prove to be a traitor after all and wind up killing Fenris? Prophecy said he would kill the wolf that destroyed Odin, but if that were true he'd be killing Logan's son.

Sylvia wasn't certain he could do that, unless…

No. It wouldn't do to start doubting now. She'd set her course and she would sail these seas no matter what.

"What do they want to know? Please tell me they didn't send us in blind."

Sylvia played with the white hair bracelet Slade had given her. "I'm not sure." Sydney whined, but Sylvia ignored it. "They said they wanted to know what she's up to, that she's been far too quiet lately."

"Huh. They're right about that." Sydney moved from the office chair and flopped down on the sofa. She pulled her feet up and wrapped her arms around her knees, a pose Sylvia had grown used to over the years. Sydney was scared, but her mind was racing. "She's been closeting herself with Henry and Luther a lot."

Sylvia grimaced. "I thought she was sleeping with them."

Sydney shot her a grin. "Well, they're doing that too, but I think they're plotting as well."

"Then we need to find out what in order to get what we want."

"Freedom." Sydney drawled the word with longing.

"Freedom." Sylvia nodded. "So. How do we do this?"

"Bug their bedroom."

Sylvia blinked. Sydney could be strangely abrupt, but her ideas usually had merit. Without Logan to protect her Sydney had been forced to come out of her shell. She was still a bit odd, but her intelligence could no longer be questioned. "Not a bad idea. We can record what we find out and hand it over to Kir and Logan."

Sydney nodded. "How, though? They lock that room up tight."

Sylvia plucked a golden hair from her head. "Leave that to me."

"Then I'll get the equipment we'll need." Sydney uncurled from the sofa. "Give me two days and I'll have everything."

"Excellent." Sylvia stretched. Somehow working with Sydney always seemed to make things better. "Pizza tonight?"

"Ugh. So tired of pizza." Sydney sat at their computer and began typing. "Chinese?"

"Thai?"

The women exchanged a glance. Sydney looked back at her screen with a grin. "Extra hot, and you're on."

Sylvia picked up the phone as her best friend began cackling like a loon. Whatever was on the screen had made her a happy woman. "Come to mama, baby. You're my little puppy now."

Sylvia shook her head. Syd was certifiable, but at least she was fun. Too bad she didn't let this side of her out when around other people. Instead she tended to revert to the meek and mild ex-wife of Loki.

Sometimes she wondered if Logan would have left if he'd seen this side of Sydney. Then again, if he hadn't left she doubted *anyone* would have seen it.

Well. At least it would be fun to watch the two of them interacting. Perhaps Sydney would be herself around all of them when this was done. Sylvia would give a lot to see Logan deal with this side of his ex.

But in the meantime, she had a lock pick to make.

Chapter Two

Magnus couldn't believe what had almost happened. Sylvia wanted to join them?

And Slade believed they were all mates?

It was as if every wish he'd ever had was finally going to be fulfilled. When the doorbell rang, he almost expected to see Sylvia on the other side, but instead it was his brother Morgan with his lover, Skye.

"You okay, bro?" Morgan tugged on Magnus's arm. "I heard something happened during your walk with Slade, but not what. Logan's been alternating between terrified and seething, and the Wonder Twins are plotting something." Morgan paused long enough to give Slade a huge hug. "Hey, brother."

Slade laughed, the husky, sweet sound going right to Magnus's cock. "Hey to you too."

Magnus rolled his eyes at his twin brother. Ever since Morgan had finally gotten the Norn of his dreams he'd been nagging Magnus to find his life partner. He'd been thrilled to find out Slade belonged to Magnus, and treated the shifter as if he were blood kin. "It's all good." He tugged Slade closer. Slade was still shaky, healing from the brutality Odin had inflicted on him. Despite his healing gift, it took a while to repair the damage done by a fucking skinning.

Skinned. Magnus shuddered. Slade had told him, in the darkness, under the covers, what Odin had done to him over and over again before they'd arrived to put a stop to it. Even thinking about it, knowing what his mate had been through while Magnus was on the Rainbow Bridge, had him seeing red. He wanted to find Odin and plant *Mjolnir* in his face a few dozen more times.

It might not kill him, but it would make *Magnus* feel a hell of a lot better.

When Odin found out Slade wasn't the loyal, mindless beast everyone had thought him to be he'd taken the man into the barn and beat him within an inch of his life, flaying the skin from him with a silver knife. He'd waited for Slade to heal, then begun all over again, removing his hide while in horse form until Slade finally broke and became a man.

Then he'd skinned the man.

It was a good thing Slade had his father's healing abilities, but not even the supernatural healing of the jotun could handle all that damage. It was leaving scars on his beautiful mate, scars that made Magnus clench his fists every time he looked at them. Odin would pay for what he had done to Sleipnir, and pay dearly. Losing Rina, his lover, was nothing compared to what he would go through when Magnus finally figured out how to kill him.

But Oliver Grimm, aka the god Odin, was a wily bastard, and not easily cornered. With the death of Rina he'd disappeared. Magnus wondered if he was busy licking his wounds the way Slade was, or if he was off plotting against them once more.

Magnus was willing to bet it was the latter. His grandfather would want to take them down even more now. He'd been fond of Rina, far more than his other lovers, and Magnus was willing to bet that her death had hit the Old Man hard.

"Slade, are you feeling any better?" Morgan's tone was soft, protective, as he entered Magnus's condo. Everyone spoke that way to Slade, as if afraid their tone alone could damage the fragile shifter.

Magnus probably appreciated that almost as much as Slade did.

"Yes, thank you." The husky tone of his soon-to-be-lover's voice was happier than he'd expected. Slade touched Magnus's chest with a smile. "Your brother is taking very good care of me." Slade leaned his head on Magnus's arm with a serene little sigh that never failed to make Magnus feel ten feet tall.

The touch of that soft, white hair, the faint brush of his hand on Magnus's arm, one look from those dark, mysterious eyes, and Magnus was putty in Slade's hands. He would do whatever it took to make sure his mate never felt another moment of pain, let alone grief.

"I hear Sylvia stopped by." Morgan crossed his arms over his chest, but Magnus could see the gesture for what it was. Morgan was worried for him. "What did she want?"

"She wants to join us." Magnus smiled as Skye, Morgan's fiancée, joined them. The Norn had lost her memory and had just gotten it back, and Morgan was as protective of her as Magnus was of Slade. "So Logan and Kir set a little test for her, to make sure she was on the up and up."

Magnus watched as Skye and Slade exchanged hugs. The two had started a tentative friendship they both seemed to enjoy.

Slade glanced over at the brothers and smiled. "They set Sif and Sygyn to spying on Frigg."

"Sylvia and Sydney, sweetheart." Slade still hadn't gotten used to calling them by their mortal names, and Magnus often found himself reminding the man what to call everyone.

"Right." Slade grimaced. "Don't worry, I'll get it eventually."

The more he spoke, the hoarser Slade's voice became. He'd spent so much time in his horse form he wasn't used to talking in his human one. "Sit down, Slade. I'll get you some tea."

The relief on Slade's face told Magnus his mate was hurting far more than he let on. Slade settled gingerly on the sofa, his gaze glued to Magnus as he chatted softly with Skye.

"Are you sure he'll be all right?" Morgan followed Magnus into the kitchen. "He should have healed fully by now. And I know I'm not the only one upset that he's not."

Magnus understood, but none of them knew the full extent of Slade's injuries. They'd all assumed that the whip was the only thing Odin had used on him, since that had been in the Old Man's hand when they'd burst into the barn. "He is, at least for now. He's finally got people willing to protect him. Let him lean on me, I can take it. I want to take it." And Magnus would, for however long Slade needed him to. He'd been abandoned, left to Grimm's non-existent mercies for centuries.

Let Slade wallow in the fact that Magnus would take care of him for as long as he needed it. When Slade was finally ready to stand on his own, Magnus would be right beside him, cheering him on. Slade's strength fascinated him, as did his innate grace, but even the strongest had times when they were weak. If Magnus was as damaged as Slade currently was, he had no doubt a healthy Slade would be just as protective, just as devoted as Magnus was toward Slade.

"And what about Sylvia?" Morgan grabbed the honey as Magnus began to prepare the tea. "Does Slade know how you feel about her?"

Magnus smiled. "He claims Sylvia belongs to us."

Morgan dropped the honey, neatly catching it before it cracked on the countertop. "He's like Fenris? I mean, one sniff and that's it?"

"Apparently." Not that Magnus was complaining.

"Whoa. You get two mates?"

"Do I detect jealousy in your tone, Morgan Tate?" Skye's voice was filled with amusement.

Morgan paled. "Of course not, dear." Morgan swirled honey in the bottom of Skye's cup with a shaking hand. "You're twice the woman Slade is."

Magnus reached up and slapped Morgan upside the head. It would have been a harder hit, except he could hear Slade laughing in the background, something he could spend the rest of his life listening to. "Asshole."

"What are we going to do to help Sylvia and Sydney?" Skye stood behind them, watching them make the tea. "I don't like the idea of them being alone in this."

"Neither do I." Slade joined them, once more leaning against Magnus. His raspy voice was worsening by the moment. "We need to help them."

"How?" Magnus settled his arm around Slade's waist while the tea steeped. "I'm more than willing to do what's necessary, especially with Skye's endorsement."

The frown on Slade's face was fierce. "We should be helping because Sylvia is ours, not because Skye said so."

Slade was right. "Sorry, love." He gazed down at his mate, and what he saw in Slade's expression sent a shiver of anticipation down his spine. "You have an idea, don't you?"

Slade nodded, his frown dissipating quickly. His mate was turning out to be remarkably practical in most things. "Yes, I do."

"Tell me, sweetheart." Magnus kissed Slade's forehead. "Tell me and I'll see that it gets done."

"Talk to Travis and Val. I'm willing to bet they'd help set up surveillance on Frigg." Slade shrugged when Magnus gaped at him. "What? I wasn't *that* far out of the loop. I know that Travis owns a detective agency, and that Val works for him now. Hell, more than once I stood there and listened to Odin gripe that Tyr wouldn't work for him anymore. Have them help. If anything, they can watch

Sylvia and Sydney as well. If they can report to Logan and Kir that the women are doing their best to uphold their end of the bargain maybe my fathers will relent and let Sylvia come to us."

Magnus grinned. "I have a stunningly beautiful, intelligent mate."

Slade preened. "Yes, you do."

He glanced over at his brother. "Morgan? What do you think?"

The look on his twin's face said it all. Morgan approved of Slade's plan. Morgan turned to his lover and kissed her softly. "Skye, stay here with Slade while we go talk to Travis and Val."

"I will." Skye put her arm around Slade. "We'll get the bedroom ready for Sylvia's arrival."

Magnus groaned as Slade nodded approvingly. "Sounds good to me." The shifter's grin was almost feral. "I want our family to be complete." And the way he eyed Magnus told him he'd better make it so.

Gods, Magnus wanted that too. Having both his lovers safe under his roof was a lifelong dream he'd never hoped to achieve. "Then let's get started. We don't want Sylvia coming home to a messy house."

Slade pulled him down for a soul-searing kiss. "Be careful, big guy." Slade patted his own ass. "Or you won't be getting any of this for a while."

Magnus moaned. "Gods, you're killing me, sweetheart." They'd done nothing more than kiss, Slade's injuries preventing anything more. Magnus was going to die of blue balls, god or no.

Slade grinned again. "Soon. I'm almost healed, and then I'm yours."

"You've been mine since the moment I heard your voice." And Magnus was slowly losing his heart to the shifter. Slade was everything Magnus had ever wanted in a male partner. His only wish was that he'd freed Slade earlier. They would still have centuries together, but Odin had stolen the past from them, time when they could have been a family.

Oh, he knew now why Slade hadn't told them what he was. He'd been protecting them, secretly, quietly, much like Logan had protected Kir. He was more like his father than he gave himself credit for.

Slade nodded. "And you've been mine." Slade gently shoved him toward the door. "Now go make sure our other mate can come home."

"Yes, sir."

Slade laughed. "I like that. I'll be herd stallion, you can be one of my mares."

Morgan, the dick, began choking on his laughter.

"Ass. Hole." Magnus grabbed hold of Morgan and dragged him toward the door. "Stop corrupting my mate."

"Me?" Morgan was still laughing as they left the condo. "You have no one to blame but yourself for that one, brother."

Magnus bit back his grin. No one else, indeed.

And that was just the way Magnus liked it.

***

Slade watched the twins walk out of the condo, smiling at how easy they were with one another. He longed for that sort of connection with his own siblings, but Fenris barely looked at him, Jörmungandr was nowhere to be found, and Hel remained in her own realm, tied there by choice now rather than caged by Odin's power. Slade had been told his father visited Helheim to ask Hel to come back with him, but she'd chosen to stay until Hodr could be released as well. Apparently the two had been lovers for centuries and had recently married with his father's blessing.

And that was another thing he was envious of. His sister and brother had been freed and found their loves, living their lives with them. Slade was still working on getting his together.

"That bad?"

"Not really." He turned to Skye with a grimace. "I'm just envious." His throat was starting to hurt now, so he finished making the tea Morgan and Magnus had started. "I want what they have." He settled down on the sofa, still unable to believe that all of this was his. He almost pulled out the key Kir had given him, the one with the peanut M&M on it, just to remind himself this was real.

He adored Magnus's condo. The clean lines of the tan sectional sofa were offset by the focus wall of polished wood. Orange curtains and pillows were the only pops of color. Even the end tables were boxy, gleaming wood that matched the wood wall the sofa was against. The glass tile around the fireplace reminded Slade of polished tiger's eye gems.

The fireplace jutted out slightly into the room. The drywall had been painted in the same orange tone as the curtains and pillows, while the mantelpiece and surround matched the wood tones of the accent wall. The rest of the walls were pale beige. The wooden floors were a lighter color than the focal wall and the end tables, contrasting them and picking up the orange tones scattered throughout the room. It was sleek and modern, yet warm at the same time. Slade loved everything about it, from the bright, cheery colors to the modern, comfortable furniture. Magnus's home was just like him, vibrant and colorful.

All it needed was the little touches Slade and Sylvia could add to make it theirs as well.

Skye sighed. "Me too, but you don't always find it."

"No, I suppose not." Skye had once been Skuld, the Norn of the Future, but she'd chosen to change the future rather than merely read it. For that, she'd been punished, her powers and memories stripped from her until Morgan found her and restored at least part of what she'd been. But a new Skuld sat where she once had, calling Urdr and Verdandi sisters. Unlike the rest of the Aesir and Vanir who'd chosen mortal names but retained their own, she'd lost the right to call herself Skuld. Skylar was now her true name, and always would be.

"So." Skye sat, her gaze seeing far more than Slade was comfortable with. "What did you really want to talk about?"

"Am I that obvious?" Slade sipped his tea gratefully. It soothed his throat, making speaking easier. Magnus might choose to believe that his voice was husky and cracked because he wasn't used to speaking as a human, but Slade knew the truth. Odin's constant abuse and Slade's centuries of screams had irreparably broken something inside him. Slade would probably never lose the reminder of what had been done to him. Not even supernatural healing could take away all of his pain.

"Yes. Now spill." Skye leaned her head on her hand, her expression eager.

"I had a couple of things on my mind, and I'm not sure where to start."

"That's easy. Start with the hard one."

He almost laughed. Easy. Slade wasn't certain he knew what easy was. He tilted his head, wondering how best to phrase what he wanted to say without sounding needy. "I want my brother to stop treating me like I'm broken."

She seemed surprised. "Really?"

He scowled. "I'm not broken, Skye. I might be bent—"

She immediately held up her hands as if to stop him. "I leave that to your mates to discover, thanks."

He rolled his eyes. "You know what I mean. I'm weak right now, I get that. I can barely stand for more than five minutes without needing to lean on something. My flesh is still knitting back together."

She slowly sat up straight. "How bad was the beating, Slade?"

He stared at her, knowing she'd be able to read his pain in his gaze. She might no longer be Skuld, but she still had power. "Jeff and I will have matching scars."

"Oh." She shivered, power flashing in her gaze. "Oh, Grimm needs to hurt."

Slade nodded. Hopefully he'd be the one to do the hurting, or at least the one to bring the popcorn and video camera. They could have family movie night.

"Have you spoken to Fenris about this?" she asked, her gaze thoughtful. "If he knew you wanted to be closer I can't imagine he'd say no."

"The only thing I can think of is he's worried about hurting me. I'm injured prey, he's *the* werewolf. Maybe that's what's wrong."

Skye frowned. "I doubt that's it, but I know a way we can find out for sure." She pulled out her cell phone and tapped something out, holding the phone away so Slade couldn't see.

Part of him knew Skye wouldn't do anything to hurt him, but… "What did you just do?"

She grinned as the doorbell rang. "Called in an expert."

Slade stood and carefully made his way to the front door. He opened it and groaned. "Aw, fuck."

Jeff Saeter gasped in outrage. "Sir! I am a married man."

"Hi, Jeff!" Skye waved as the red-haired mate of Slade's brother gently pushed past him.

Jeff was a shorter version of Magnus and Morgan, less broad in the shoulder but with the same twinkling gaze and vibrant personality. He'd been the first one to hug Slade hard, ignoring the outburst from the rest of the family. He'd somehow known that Slade needed to be held tight. "Hey, sweetie." Jeff bent over and kissed the Norn on the cheek. "Where's my brother?"

"Which one?"

"Either." Jeff flopped onto the sofa, snarling when his hair landed under his butt. "Stupid wolf."

Slade glanced at Skye. He'd already heard the grumbles about how Fenris, who worshiped Jeff's red curls, had willed them to grow. Jeff was now unable to cut his hair short. It would simply grow back overnight. The women of the family were teaching him how to deal with the unruly mane, and while Jeff grumbled Slade could see the pleasure he tried to hide. The fact that Fenris loved him so deeply kept the grumbles to just that, nothing but good-natured bellyaching.

Still, Slade wasn't about to pass up an opportunity to tease his brother-in-law. "What's he an expert on, crème rinse?"

Jeff eyed him with a cheeky grin. "I always wanted to ask you something."

"What?" Slade had a bad feeling about this.

"Are you really hung like a horse?"

Dead silence filled the room as Skye and Slade stared at Jeff.

Finally, Slade allowed a slow smile to cross his face as he leaned back against the door. "Jealous?"

Jeff cleared his throat and crossed his legs, his cheeks turning red. "Nope."

Slade moved away from the door, aware he was going to fall down soon if he didn't sit down. The skin might be intact now, but the nerve endings beneath were still off-kilter. It made every movement painful and sometimes disorienting. "So. Skye tells me you're the authority on all things Fenris." He sat next to Jeff, trying to look casual.

"That *would* be me." And Jeff looked very pleased by that fact. "What can I do you for?"

Slade chuckled. "Honey, you couldn't afford me."

Jeff looked shocked, then laughed. "As long as Magnus can, then I'm happy."

"He can." Slade couldn't help the soft smile any more than the blush.

Jeff took hold of his hand. "In case I haven't made it clear, I'm happy for both of you."

"Thanks." Slade took a deep breath. "But that's not why Skye texted you."

"Oh." Jeff squeezed his hand. "This has to do with Fen, doesn't it?"

Slade decided to bite the bullet. "Why is he avoiding me? Is it because I'm hurt and he's afraid he'll eat me?"

Jeff's eyes went wide. "What? No!" Jeff sighed, running his hand through his thick curls. His hair was so long Slade could touch the tips without lifting his hand off the sofa. "Fen is giving you time."

"Time? What for?" Slade was confused.

"To heal, and bond with your mate." Jeff took Slade's hands in his. "He's all torn up inside, thinking that he barely knew you. Hell, he told me he ignored you because he thought you were…"

"A mistake." Slade allowed that old pain to flow over him. The unwanted child, given away before he'd barely taken his first wobbly steps. It had taken him centuries to figure out it wasn't his fault, that he'd done nothing wrong. Hell, it had taken another century after *that* to realize that Logan hadn't done anything wrong either. Grimm had demanded Sleipnir and, thinking Sleipnir would have a good life with Odin, he'd been handed over. But not without a qualm or two, and certainly not without wishing that Sleipnir could have more than Logan could provide.

Jeff nodded reluctantly. "In a way, yes. You were an animal, intelligent for one, but still nothing more than a beast. And for him, I think you represented what he could have been if things had turned out differently."

But that wasn't Slade's fault. It had never been.

"I know." Jeff responded as if he'd said those words out loud. "And I'm working on him, I promise. He's taking this almost as hard as Logan did."

"But Papa speaks to me. Fenris doesn't."

"And if you don't breach that gap you're worried you might never grow closer?"

Slade nodded.

"Then come to breakfast tomorrow morning." Skye piped in, startling Slade. He'd been so focused on Jeff he'd almost forgotten she was there. "Make sure you sit next to him and talk to him. If necessary Jeff and I will help."

Jeff nodded. "Confronting him head-on might be the best way to deal with him if you were healed, but this might work as well." He shrugged. "It's worth a shot, anyway, until I can pull his head out from between his ass cheeks."

Slade cocked an eyebrow. "I thought his head was between your ass cheeks."

Jeff smiled. "And I'm very happy to have it there." He waggled his brows. "When I'm not thinking about Vincente, that is."

Slade tilted his head. "Who's Vincente?"

Skye groaned.

Jeff rubbed his hands together and cackled evilly. "Oh, you precious baby. Just you wait and see."

Suddenly, Slade was very, very afraid.

Chapter Three

"Oh dear."

Sylvia looked up from her book to see Syd biting her lip. "What?"

"I just got an email from Frederica. She wants to meet us today."

Sylvia put down her book, her heart pounding with fear. "Do you think she knows?"

"How? You only met with them this morning." But Syd looked just as worried as Sylvia felt.

"I have no idea." Sylvia bit her lip, her mind racing over the possibilities. Frederica didn't have the same ability to keep tabs on the Aesir and Vanir that Grimm had. The ravens only answered to him, and now that he was no longer a part of Frederica's life she couldn't ask him to look for her. So unless she had someone following them, there was no way she could know that they were trying to join Kir. "No. I think we're okay."

"Then maybe it has something to do with why she's been consulting so much with Henry and Luther." Syd turned back to her computer, clicking away at whatever it was Syd did. Sylvia had long ago stopped asking what her friend did to earn human money. The lengthy explanation had made her head hurt.

"So you think Logan and Kir are right and she's up to something."

Syd shrugged. "She tried to get her hands on *Mjolnir*, and I don't think it was because she wanted a memento."

"Hmm." Sylvia turned that over in her mind. "She wants Logan dead in the worst way, and Kir back at her side."

Syd nodded, her attention mostly on her screen. "It's possible Luther or Henry thought they could wield it since they also share Thor's blood."

"But the prophecy states *Mjolnir* will be held by Magni and Modi. And with the two of them following Kir…" It just didn't make sense.

"Then whatever she had planned for *Mjolnir* fell through when the brothers found it." Syd turned in her chair, finally invested in the conversation. "That means she's going to implement Plan B."

"Because she always has a Plan B." Sylvia stared at Syd in horror.

Syd nodded. "And Plan B involves the ex-wives of Loki and Thor."

Sylvia closed her eyes. "They aren't going to believe this wasn't the plan all along."

Syd sighed. "It's possible I'm wrong. She might just be planning a trip to Tahiti and wants us to water her plants."

Sylvia rolled her eyes. "Oh, sure, because mistletoe requires such personal attention."

Syd chuckled. "Okay, maybe not. There's no use worrying over what she wants until we find out."

"I think we should go pick up the surveillance equipment tonight. This might be our best chance to get it into place." Sylvia stood and grabbed her purse.

"Sounds good." Syd followed, grabbing her own purse and following Sylvia out the door. "I have the list of what we need on my tablet. It shouldn't be difficult, especially since I know where Travis shops for his stuff."

Sylvia was the one with a car, so she drove. Syd had a bad habit of getting lost in thought even behind the wheel, so she generally took taxis or the bus everywhere. It was one of the many reasons Sylvia had chosen to live with Syd, because the woman had a hard time with the necessities of life. Put her in front of her computer and she was a genius.

Put her in front of the wheel, and Mayhem became jealous of the amount of damage she could do in so little time.

"Where to?" Sylvia pulled out of the apartment complex's parking lot and onto the street.

Syd quietly gave directions, and before long they were in front of a little shopping area full of electronics stores. Syd got out first and headed directly for a shop called Kerkelly Security. She opened the door, holding it for Sylvia.

An older human with salt-and-pepper hair and kind brown eyes smiled at them. "Can I help you ladies?"

Sylvia stepped up to the counter and smiled back. "We're looking for help."

The man's smile dimmed. "What's the problem?"

Syd glanced at Sylvia before pointing toward the case. "We need some surveillance equipment. We think our ex-mother-in-law is stealing from us, but the police won't believe us without proof, so we want to bug our house and see if we can catch her in the act."

The man nodded as if he'd heard a similar story before. "So you need things like a nanny-cam?"

"Exactly." Syd smiled at the man, and the two began talking megapixels and download times and blah blah blah until Sylvia's eyes crossed. All the electronic crap bored her spitless. Give her a remote control and she could figure out how to work the television, but that was about it.

When Syd was *finally* happy with her purchases she led the way back out of the shop and climbed into the passenger seat. "Now all I have to do is install a little gift in Frederica's root directory and set up the nanny-cam in her bedroom and we're golden."

Sylvia blinked. "Do I want to know how you're going to do all of that?"

"Nope."

"Will it get us what we want?"

"It will give us direct access to her ingoing and outgoing traffic, so…" Syd shrugged.

"That would be a yup." Sylvia made the turn into Frederica's driveway. "Is it illegal?"

"Yup."

"All righty then." She pulled up in front of the double doors of the Grimm mansion, aware Frederica was already watching them. Now that her brain was no longer fried by apple juice cocktails, Frederica was back to being the evil bitch they'd all known and hated so long ago. "How do we do it?"

"I'll take care of that, you just figure out what the hell she wants and how we're going to survive this."

Sylvia could do that. She was the warrior of the pair. Now that she had a chance to get out from under Frederica and the Old Man she was more than willing to fight for it.

The front door opened as they got out of the car. Frederica stood on the top step, no longer the granny they'd become accustomed to. Instead, her shoes were four-inch red stilettos and her white suit was Versace, with a red silky top beneath it. Her blonde hair had been trimmed into a long, sleek bob with nary a strand out of place. Her makeup was flawlessly professional, just the right amount of color and shine for a woman who ran a multi-million dollar corporation.

If she'd been a different sort of person Sylvia might have admired her. But Frederica's single-minded determination to destroy Logan and Jordan Tate-Saeter and restore Kiran Tait to her side had driven a wedge between them that nothing but Frederica's surrender could remove.

That would happen when Frederica's flying monkeys learned the fox trot.

Syd flinched at the hint of a scowl on Frederica's face, and Sylvia straightened her spine. Better Frederica's ire be directed at her. Syd couldn't handle that kind of heat. "Frederica."

Frederica, once Frigg and queen of the Aesir and Vanir, sniffed. "You're late."

"Traffic." Syd spoke quietly, a pale mouse in front of a lion.

Frederica's brows rose, but she didn't question them further. "Follow me."

She turned on one delicate heel and marched back into her mausoleum of a home.

Syd shot Sylvia a worried glance before following Frederica. "Um, Frederica?"

Frederica sighed. "What is it?"

"Bathroom."

Frederica waved, but continued to head toward the sitting room. "You know where it is."

"Thanks." Syd nodded to Sylvia and took off toward where one of the downstairs bathrooms was. Once Sylvia had Frederica distracted, Syd would do whatever it was Syd had in mind.

It was Sylvia's job to make sure she got to do it.

She followed Frederica into the sitting room, settling into a chair at Frederica's wave. "What did you want, Frederica?"

The woman smiled grimly. "I want you to spy on my son."

Oh, fuck. She'd guessed right for once.

"Or, more specifically, I want Syd to." Frederica sat gingerly on her elaborate Victorian chaise and held up a tea pot. "Earl Grey?"

"Please." She waited patiently while Frederica poured the tea, adding cream the way Sylvia preferred. She picked up the cup and sipped, nodding her appreciation at the warm, creamy flavor. As Frederica poured her own cup, Sylvia set hers down. "So. What exactly did you need Syd to do?"

"I want her to hack into Logan Saeter's computer files and find something that will make my son want to leave him once and for all."

Sylvia's brows rose. From what she could tell Logan could set the house on fire and Kir would merely yawn and put it out.

"Where is Sydney?" Frederica frowned at the doorway.

"Ah." Sylvia had to think fast. "We had cheese omelets for breakfast, and—"

Frederica held up her hand and shuddered delicately. "No need to say any more." She huffed impatiently. "The girl knows she's lactose intolerant."

Sylvia ignored Frederica's grimace. "What makes you think there's anything on Logan's computer that will piss off Kir?"

She didn't like the way Frederica eyed her. Cold, calculating, and with a hint of disdain, the woman's look sent a chill down Sylvia's spine. "She'll find something." Frederica sat back, a smile on her face that reminded Sylvia of a cat. "Trust me."

Sylvia nodded. "All right. I'll speak to Syd, find out—"

"Find out what?" Syd entered the room timidly, her gaze grazing Frederica before landing firmly on Sylvia.

"If you can hack Logan's computer." No sense in hiding what Frederica wanted. That might make Frederica suspicious, and they didn't need that right now.

"Oh." Syd seemed to shrink in on herself. "I think I can."

"Good. I'll email you the details of what I want, and when I want it by."

Frederica didn't stand, but Sylvia knew a dismissal when she heard one.

She stood and took hold of Syd's shaking hand. "We'll wait for your instructions."

Before Frederica could respond Sylvia and Syd were out the front door. "Shit shit double shit." Sylvia slid behind the wheel and slammed the car door shut.

Syd slid into the passenger seat, making sure she closed the door before turning to Sylvia. "We have to tell them."

"You think?" Sylvia started the car and drove carefully down the long driveway. She didn't want Frederica to catch on to how nervous she was.

"In other news, I got what we needed taken care of."

That was a relief. "No one saw you?"

"Do they ever?" Syd shrugged. "Not that I'm aware of."

"Good. Then let's get out of here."

***

Frederica watched out the window as the two women drove away. Something had been off about them. Sydney had always been shy and retiring, but today she'd been almost nonexistent. And Sylvia had been far too accommodating and eager to please.

No. They were up to something, but for the life of her Frederica couldn't figure out what.

"Love?" Henry sidled up behind her and put his arm around her waist. "Did you speak to them?"

"Did they agree?" Luther's deeper tones surrounded her, made her shiver.

Henry and Luther. The brothers of Odin—Vili, now known as Henry Grimm, and Ve, aka Luther Grimm—were the only reason she hadn't completely lost herself to the rage that had built in her as her traitorous husband's apple toddies wore off. "They did, but..."

Luther took hold of her hand as Henry's arms tightened around her. "But?"

"There was something wrong with the way they reacted. I expected an argument, or at least questions, but they couldn't leave here fast enough."

"It's a shame Sydney is the best at computer hacking. She still has feelings for Logan." Luther squeezed her hand. "Can you think of anyone who would do the work instead?"

Henry kissed the side of her neck, and Frederica tilted her head so he'd have better access. "Even if they aren't as good, at least they might be loyal."

"You think they'll betray me?" Frederica thought her lovers might be on to something.

"It's a possibility you need to consider, yes." Luther turned her to face him, cupping her cheeks between his palms. His strength, his warmth held her steady in an increasingly rocky world. "The only other option is to accept—"

"No." Frederica wouldn't even think about it. "Baldur needs to return home."

"Shh." Henry moved to stand next to his brother. "You know Luther only has your best interests at heart."

"I hate seeing you so unhappy." Luther stroked her hair back, his expression filled with his love.

How had she ever looked at Odin and thought he cared? Luther and Henry had proven over and over what she was to them. She would forever be grateful to that cheating, lying whoreson for leaving her with them. "I know, love." She returned his caress, smiling up at her lovers equally. "No. We'll find another way. I will have everything I want."

The brothers exchanged a glance, and she knew. She knew they didn't quite believe, but she did. None of them were listed in the Edda as dying.

They would live. And she would have Kir and Holden back again.

***

"So, what do you think?" Magnus watched Val and Travis, hoping the two men would agree. It was a little much to ask, but he had the feeling Travis, at least, would be sympathetic. He'd called them to Morgan's apartment, unwilling to bring Logan and Kir into this. He wanted to give Sylvia the benefit of the doubt and prove to them that what she'd asked for was actually what she wanted.

The two men glanced at one another. Travis was the first to speak. "I think we can do it, but it will take a little time to set up."

Val nodded. "Unfortunately, I'll have to do my part from a distance." He grimaced. "Sydney is terrified of me for some reason."

Travis's brows rose. "Maybe because you tried to kill Logan multiple times."

"I didn't mean it." Val rolled his eyes. "Some people really need to get over that."

"Tell that to Sydney."

"Yeah, yeah." Val grunted in disgust. "Geez. Blow someone up a couple of times and suddenly you're a bad guy." He glanced over at Travis. "How will we do it without alerting them that we're watching? Syd is really good with computers. She'll detect it if we try to hack into her system."

"Long distance surveillance. Break out the van, watch their condo. Move them in immediately if it looks like Frederica or Grimm are on to them." Travis picked up his phone. "I'll call in the cavalry and get Jeff to help."

"If you've got Jeff you've also got Fenris." Magnus knew *he* wouldn't let his mate out on a job without protection, namely himself. Fenris was twice as overprotective as Magnus, especially since the Old Man had tried to skin Jeff. If Jeff so much as set a toe outside his condo the wolf knew it.

Val scowled. "We haven't heard anything from dear old Daddy since he got the snot beat out of him. Any idea what he's up to? I'd hate to forget about him while focusing on Freddie."

Freddie? Magnus snorted. "If she heard you call her that she'd rip your spleen out through your asshole."

Val grinned viciously. "She could try."

"You don't need to concern yourself with Grimm."

Magnus jumped. That voice came from everywhere and nowhere and was as familiar as his own. "Heimdall?"

A pair of icy, glowing eyes appeared, followed by the man himself. "Magni. I hear you're looking for Grimm."

"Among other things." He shouldn't be surprised that Heimdall had heard them. The Guardian of the Bifrost Bridge, Nik DeWitt, aka Heimdall, could see and hear anything he wished to simply by focusing on it. What did surprise him was the fact that Nik was *here*. "How did you get through Logan's wards?"

Nik merely smiled. He should have known Nik wouldn't answer. "I'm willing to help you, but I want something in return."

Magnus and Morgan shared a look. Nik's help could be invaluable in getting Sylvia and Sydney moved in, but the cost might be something they weren't willing to pay. "What do you want?"

Nik's smile sent shivers down his spine. "I want Toni moved in tomorrow."

Magnus blinked. "That…might be harder than you think." The cop had refused every offer to move in, even after Fenris had declared her family. She'd saved Jeff's life, healing him when nothing else had worked. They'd been surprised to find she had Valkyrie blood in her, but Nik had probably known all along. Hell, he probably knew what color underwear Magnus was wearing.

Nik was one of the few gods, Aesir or Vanir, who scared the fuck out of Magnus.

"She's in danger. Move her in, and I'll help you. Refuse, and I won't." Nik leaned forward, and for a moment Magnus saw the dark-haired, crystal-eyed god rather than the suave lawyer Nik pretended to be. "Trust me. You want my help, Magni, son of Thor."

Magnus gritted his teeth. By calling him that, Nik had made the request a formal one from one god to another. "I'll do my best."

His best might involve a felony, but he'd get Toni here before the end of the day.

Nik nodded and disappeared.

There was silence in Morgan's condo as the Guardian's disappearing act left Magnus reeling. "How did he do that?"

"I don't know." Travis frowned thoughtfully at the spot where Nik had been standing. "He's always been a mystery, even to me."

Since Travis, also known as the god Tyr, had once been the Lord of the Vanir, that was saying something. Tyr had lost the war Odin had started, handing over the Godspear as a war prize. Under the influence of Idunn's apples and Grimm's influence, he'd quietly become one of Grimm's staunchest supporters, even sacrificing his own hand to imprison his foster son, Fenrisùlfr, son of Loki. Once out from under that influence, he'd married Jamie Grimm and become one of Kir's fiercest protectors. He'd been the one to free Fenris and bring Jeff and Fenris together.

Fenris was finally forgiving him, and there was little Travis wouldn't do for the werewolf.

"How do we get Toni here?" Morgan ran his hands through his bright red hair, so similar to his own that Magnus almost felt it. His twin looked exactly like him except for the easier smile around his eyes and a slightly clearer sapphire blue in his gaze. Magnus's eyes had a slight hint of green in them that edged him toward turquoise.

"You two deal with that." Val pointed toward Travis. "We'll set up surveillance on Syd and Sylvia."

"Thanks." Magnus had the feeling they had the easier job. Getting the cop moved in was going to be a pain in the ass.

"I say we drug her."

Magnus stared at his brother. He could not have heard that correctly.

"What? Can you think of a way to get her here without hurting her? Because I can't."

"Are you serious?" Magnus was going to smack his twin. "She'll feed us our balls."

Morgan looked smug. "Not if we lock her in her condo before she wakes up."

Magnus tried to find the flaw in his twin's plan. "That could work."

Travis sighed. "I have a better idea than felony kidnapping. Why don't you call her and ask her to come here to talk? Tell her about Slade, ask her to look at him and hear his story. Then tell her about Nik. Maybe if we tell her that her life might be in danger she'll listen."

Magnus wasn't so sure. "Toni is pretty stubborn."

Val piped up. "She's a cop. If we tell her she's there to protect Slade, she might do it."

"She'll lose her job. She's a homicide detective, remember?" Travis rubbed his chin. "Let me pull some strings, see if I can get her here without having to fight her." He grimaced. "All right, Plan B. You two take Fen, Jeff and the van and set up the surveillance. Val will get

Logan to set up Toni's condo while I work on getting Toni here."

Val nodded and left, waving good-bye to Magnus and Morgan on his way out.

"Let's go tell Slade and Skye we're heading out." Morgan clapped his hand on Magnus's shoulder. "Your mate should be thrilled."

Hell, Magnus was too. Watching Sylvia beat the hell out of trying to get a reluctant homicide cop to move in. "We'll get Jeff to show Fenris how to set up the equipment."

"Good idea." Travis pulled out his cell phone, heading out of the condo with them. "It's about time I put the furball on the payroll."

"Logan might have something to say about that." Magnus wasn't certain Logan wouldn't pitch a fit of epic proportions. When it came to his kids, the man was a lunatic.

Then again, Grimm had tortured them all and murdered one of them, so he had a reason to be.

Travis shrugged. "If we tell him it's for Slade, he'll be all right with it."

Magnus doubted it, but Fenris was a grown man. If he accepted Travis's offer, he could deal with Logan. There wasn't much Logan wouldn't do to make his children happy.

Magnus never thought he'd say this, but he was glad his half-sister, Jordan, had married the jotun. Logan and Kir were going to be stellar fathers to her twins.

Magnus waved good-bye to Travis as he opened the door to his condo. His eyes went wide as the familiar, gut-clenching sounds filled the air. Three heads, two blond and one curly red, were huddled together over a laptop, the intent expressions on their faces causing Magnus to groan.

"Oh, hell." Morgan groaned. "Jeff's introducing them to Vincente."

"Mm, Vincente," Jeff moaned.

Slade whimpered, his gaze glued to the screen. "Why did I not know of this man?"

Magnus scowled. Slade shouldn't make those kinds of sounds over anyone but him and Sylvia.

Jeff turned and stared at Slade. "Living in a barn for centuries? Lousy cable service in Asgard? Or how about having a skeezeweasel for a master?"

Slade didn't even turn as he shot Jeff the finger. Slade licked his lips, and Magnus was ready to send Jeff's laptop out the window.

Skye looked over both their heads and mouthed at Morgan *"help me"*.

Magnus walked over and plucked Slade off the sofa. "I think it's time someone took a nap."

Slade sighed dramatically as he cuddled into Magnus. "Damn. And Vincente was just about to take off his pants."

Oh, that was it. Jeff's computer was going to meet its tech god.

Slade petted Magnus's chest. "How do you feel about gold lamé briefs?"

Chapter Four

Slade chuckled as Magnus growled at Jeff. The man looked ready to pounce on the poor, defenseless laptop and maul it to pieces. "Down boy."

Those brilliant green eyes turned toward him and he shivered. The heat in his mate's gaze was burning him up. "You shouldn't want anyone but your mates, Sleipnir."

Oh, someone was pissed. Magnus was the one who insisted on using mortal names. The use of Slade's jotun name told him exactly how serious Magnus was. Slade lowered his gaze submissively, enjoying the way Magnus's chest rumbled against him. "Yes, Magni."

"We'll be right back." Magnus's gaze darted toward the bedroom door, and Slade shivered.

Morgan must have known exactly what his twin had in mind, because he took hold of Skye and started walking toward the front door. "C'mon, Jeff. Let's go talk to Fenris."

Jeff picked up the laptop and followed. "Only if I can bring Vincente."

Whatever Morgan said in reply went unheard. Slade had far more important things on his mind than Vincente.

Magnus kissed him, but instead of the sweet, gentle kisses they'd shared before, this one was hot, claiming, demanding that Slade submit to Magnus's desires. Magnus had been so careful with him, so gentle while he healed, that Slade hadn't realized he could even kiss like this.

Slade wanted more. This heat, this passion, the knowledge that Magnus was so fiercely possessive that he would almost forget that Slade was injured? It was far more drugging than anything Jeff could show him on his laptop.

Slade wrapped his arms around Magnus's neck, thrilled when the big man began to move. Magnus carried him into the bedroom, not even acknowledging the fact that Morgan, Skye and Jeff had all left.

They banged into the wall next to the bedroom door, sending Slade into a fit of giggles.

Magnus lifted his mouth from Slade's with a groan. "This works a whole lot better in the movies."

Slade nodded, still laughing as Magnus lowered him to the huge California king bed. "I hate to tell you this, but Richard Gere you ain't." He settled down with a happy sigh. He'd never thought he'd get to live somewhere so *warm*.

Slade would have kept the man for this room alone. There was just one thing about it that bothered him.

"What are you thinking about so hard?" Magnus pulled off his shirt, showing off a lightly furred chest that made Slade want to purr and rub himself all over it. Slade hadn't dared do more than touch Magnus's bare chest, afraid he'd start something neither of them could finish.

"Mmm." Slade stretched, loving the way Magnus's eyes glazed over with lust. "Ceilings."

Magnus blinked. "Ceilings."

Slade nodded and tried not to laugh. Teasing Magnus was becoming one of his favorite pastimes. "I think yours should be beige."

Magnus's eyes narrowed.

"I think it would make the room more comf—" Slade suddenly found his lips occupied as Magnus pounced on him, kissing him again. Ceilings were forgotten as Magnus ravaged his mouth, reminding him that beds were for more than sleeping in.

Gods, it had been so long since Slade had done more than sleep in a bed. Hell, he hadn't done much more than rub off against someone else, too terrified that Odin would figure out that he was more than just a dumb, defenseless animal, eager to do his bidding. He'd never had the opportunity to slide between crisp sheets and mess them up with a lover. Slade had never had someone make love to him before.

He planned on changing that before the night was over.

Magnus removed the rest of his clothes quickly, and then began carefully removing Slade's shirt. He slid it over Slade's skin in a slow, sensual glide, kissing each and every scrape and scar that Odin had left behind. The Old Man had worked him over, and Slade had the bruises to prove it. The soft feel of Magnus's lips sliding over his skin distracted him from the mottled look of his flesh.

He would heal. He'd be scarred, but the bruises would fade. It was far more important to get the scent of Magnus on his skin, to taste and tease and prove that he was alive and free.

He lifted up and allowed Magnus to pull the shirt completely off, smiling slightly when it hit the floor. "What was that about ceilings?"

Slade chuckled. "Nothing, dear." He'd revisit the idea later, when he didn't have other things to occupy his mind and his hands.

Magnus, despite the hunger Slade could clearly see in his gaze, was still careful of Slade's wounds. He watched Slade's expression as he carefully removed Slade's pants, searching for any signs of discomfort.

Slade was terrified that Magnus would stop if he so much as flinched. Years of hiding himself from everyone came to his rescue as he made sure Magnus didn't suspect he was still in pain. Slade would rather experience the discomfort of his jeans brushing over the marks on his legs than have Magnus stop.

"Are you sure you're up for this?" Magnus rubbed his hand over Slade's calf. "We can wait if you're not ready yet."

"Do it and die." Slade glared at Magnus. "I swear if I beat off one more time my hand will fall off." Just smelling Magnus's scent on the sheets was enough to make his dick hard. Having Magnus naked and at his mercy?

Slade was already close to coming, and he'd barely been touched.

Magnus studied him for a long moment, making Slade nervous as hell. "You're right arm is a little bigger than your left, now that I think about it."

"Magnus."

Magnus took hold of his right hand and examined his fingers one by one, touching each of them. "And you do seem to have calluses on your hand."

"I will seriously end you." As much as Slade loved the playful side of Magnus, now was so not the time.

When Magnus poked Slade's cock, Slade hoped they'd finally get this show on the road. "It does look a little red and angry there."

"I swear, if you don't suck, I'll blow."

Magnus's eyes sparkled with laughter.

Slade glared back. "And not in the good way."

Magnus grinned. "Any other demands while you're at it?"

Slade tilted his head, thinking about it. "Yup."

"What?" Magnus stroked Slade's cock, and Slade's eyes crossed.

"Could we do this before I die of old age?" Slade could barely speak, his voice cracking as Magnus ran his tongue over the head of his cock.

"You're immortal, remember?"

"Exactly!"

Magnus leaned his head on Slade's thigh and laughed.

Slade whimpered in frustration, his head banging against the pillows. "You're killing me here."

"Sorry." Magnus more than made up for it when he finally, thank you gods, took Slade's cock in his mouth. "Is that better?"

"It was." Slade pointed toward his now wet dick. "Finish him!"

Magnus looked like he was having far too much fun for a man who was *not* sucking Slade's cock. "You've been playing video games again."

Like Slade had much more to do while he healed. "Magnus Tate, I swear to…oh…"

He never got to finish the threat. Magnus swallowed him down to the root, something no other lover had ever managed to do before. He had a brief second to be furiously jealous before Magnus began to suck him in earnest, bringing Slade quickly to the brink of explosion. "Please." He began babbling, barely aware of what he was croaking out as his vision blurred and the pleasure overwhelmed his senses.

When Magnus's finger breached him, Slade cracked, thrusting into Magnus's mouth with a fierceness that startled them both. This was his mate whose mouth was on him, his mate who was giving him everything, and Slade took it, cupping the back of Magnus's head with greedy fingers. He wanted it all, wanted the burn of being breached, the warm, wet heat that surrounded him. He wanted, needed, to feel his mate's passion for him, to know that nothing could take Magnus from him.

He'd kill any who tried.

Slade screamed, the orgasm washing over him so strong he thought he might black out. He poured himself into Magnus's mouth, the force of the ecstasy shuddering through him. When it finally ended, when he was spent and limp and panting for breath, Magnus was there, holding him close as he burst into surprised tears.

"Shh. It's okay, Slade. I understand."

He probably did. Magnus knew what it was like to go from unwanted burden to desired lover. "Thank you." For so much more than the orgasm, but Slade didn't say it. He didn't have to. Magnus understood without the words.

He proved it by hugging Slade tightly. "You're welcome."

After a few moments Magnus rolled over and plucked a knife off the bedside table. "I want to bond with you."

Slade blinked away more tears. "Are you sure?"

Magnus smiled sweetly and slashed his palm. "Blood to blood, you are mine."

"Blood to blood." Slade held up his shaking hand, barely feeling it when Magnus gave him a shallow cut. "Thank you."

Magnus blew him a kiss and pressed their palms together. "Mine."

Slade shuddered as the warmth of his lover seeped into him.

***

"Any luck?" Sylvia stretched, pulling the headphones from her ears. They'd set up to record anything that was heard, but Sylvia was afraid they'd miss something that was immediately dangerous to either themselves or Logan, so she'd chosen the boring task of listening to the goings-on in the Grimm mansion. So far, she'd heard nothing more than the everyday conversations she'd expect in any household, along with the deep affection Henry and Luther held for Frederica.

Hell. If the goddess would just give up her obsession with destroying Logan maybe she could live a happy life with her lovers. But Frederica had never been known as a woman who walked away from something she saw as a personal injury. She still, after so many years, believed Logan was bad for her son.

Talk about the mother-in-law from hell. Humans might complain about their MILs, but Frederica really would put a curse on Logan if she could. Sylvia spared a brief thought for the long-dead Nanna, Kir's wife when he still lived his life as the god Baldur, who'd been forced to put up with the woman during her marriage to him.

"No, but I expected it to take some time." Sydney's tone was absent as she tapped away at her keyboard. "I'm working on hacking Logan's computer first."

"Why? I thought we'd do Frederica's." Sylvia didn't always understand how Sydney's mind worked, but the woman knew what she was doing when it came to computers.

"We're capturing her incoming and outgoing traffic. I'm saving everything to go over later. That was the easy part, once I got to her computer. Nope. Breaking Logan's security is the real challenge."

Someone was having way too much fun. Sydney was practically cackling with glee as she typed. "Okay." Sylvia stood, the Thai they'd had for dinner long since gone. "Want a snack?"

"Sure. Do we have any more of that Greek yogurt you got last Monday?"

"I think so." It was Sydney's favorite snack, so Sylvia made sure to keep it on hand. She carried back two yogurts and two glasses of water. "Here you go."

"Thanks." Sydney took both the drink and the snack. "I'm still not sure what Frederica hopes to find."

"You think she planted something on Logan's computer?"

"Pfft." Sydney shook her head. "Please. I'm the best she's got, and I know *I* didn't break through Logan's security to put something there. She doesn't have anyone else with near the skill I've got."

"She could have used her powers, cast a spell on something." Sydney frowned thoughtfully. "Done right, all it would take is an email attachment."

"Logan wouldn't open anything from Frederica."

"No, but would he open something from Nik or Kye, or even me?" Sydney shrugged. "All she'd need is the passwords for their email accounts."

"I suppose." Damn, it was possible Frederica had done just that. Nik DeWitt and Kye Vanderale, Heimdall and Njord respectively, had both been on the books at Grimm and Sons. Frederica would have access to those accounts now that she'd taken over the business. "But what could she put on there that would be bad enough to get Kir to leave Logan and go home to her?"

Sydney bit her lip. "Proof of infidelity."

Sylvia let that idea roll around for a bit. What she remembered of Baldur was a sweet-natured man, easily laughing, but not one to be trifled with when his anger was roused. If he could be convinced that Logan had been unfaithful, that anger might be enough to push Logan out into the cold before reason reestablished itself. "What should we do? Should we tell them?"

Sydney shook her head. "Let me see if I can find anything first. I could be wrong, but it's the only thing I can think of that could break them up."

"Do you think your hacking could set off whatever it is she planted?" Sylvia had no idea if that was even possible, but she wouldn't put anything past Frederica. The spell could be keyed to a hacking attempt, which would be why she'd set Sydney and Sylvia to finding it rather than waiting for Kir to find it.

"I…don't know." For the first time Sylvia looked alarmed. "I suppose that's possible. Normally, if I was dealing with a human, I'd say no, but…" She shrugged. "She's crafty enough to set it up that way."

"I might be paranoid, but that's what I would do. I mean, it's obvious to anyone who sees them how deeply Logan loves Kir and Jordan. There's no way he'd do anything to jeopardize his relationship with them."

"We have to hope, then, that Kir would see a trap."

"Not if she spelled it correctly."

Sydney was beginning to frighten Sylvia. "Oh, shit." If Frederica put the spell on the attachment in such a way that Kir would be under its influence rather than, say, Logan, it could mean disaster. Kir would react as if he believed the evidence, even if it was wildly implausible. "We definitely need to warn them, even if they don't believe us."

"What if we get to their place and there's nothing on Logan's computer? What then?" Sydney stood, throwing out her trash and picking up her purse. For all she was protesting, she obviously planned on going through with it.

"Then we tell them what Frederica is up to and have them help listen in on her." Sydney grabbed her own purse, ready to head out.

Before she could get two steps, the lights went out. "Crap."

"I'll get the flashlight."

Sydney might be calm, but Sylvia was freaking the hell out. "There's no storm."

"Huh?"

Sylvia could hear Syd rummaging around for the flashlight, cursing softly. "I said, there's no storm. Why did the lights go out?"

Silence. "Oh, fuck."

Sylvia nodded, even though she knew Syd couldn't see her. "We need to get out."

Syd whimpered. "You think it's Val?"

"He has no reason to come after us, Syd." She really needed to get over her fear of the Avenger. If she did, she might be able to figure out a way to get the man to notice her.

"If he thinks we really are working for Frederica, he does." The click of the flashlight and the sudden burst of light had her blinking. "Let's go."

Sylvia followed Sydney, her senses on high alert. There was no way they could fight Val or Odin or Henry, or hell, anyone. Neither of them were warriors. Thor had protected her when they'd been married, even when he was unfaithful. After their divorce, there'd been no need for warriors, as the advent of modern times meant Sylvia felt relatively safe within the boundaries Odin had set for them. Hell, even after the Old Man had been defeated and the apples of Idunn put under lock and key, she'd felt safe.

Now that sense of safety mocked her. She tiptoed toward her front door, terrified out of her mind. Her heart was pounding, her palms sweating, the fear causing every little creak to sound twice as loud as it really was. "Syd?"

"Yeah?" Syd reached for the door handle.

"Be careful." Syd was even less ready for a confrontation than Sylvia was.

"Sure thing." But Sydney's voice was shaking, the light from the flashlight moving erratically. Her friend was just as terrified as she was.

After a deep, cleansing breath, Syd opened the front door and took a look around. "No one there."

"Good. Let's go." Sylvia put her hand on Syd's shoulder, more than ready to get the hell out of Dodge.

When a hand landed on *her* shoulder, she shrieked so loud she was certain she woke up Hel.

Chapter Five

"He cried?" Morgan took off the headphones, his expression surprised. He set down the headphones and began to laugh. "He seriously had a crymax?"

Magnus smacked his brother hard. "Dickhead. At least I know my kitchen table is safe to eat off of."

Morgan only laughed harder. "Mama always said we should eat at the table."

Magnus rolled his eyes and tried to ignore his idiot twin. He had more important things to worry about. "I don't think Slade's had any real affection in his entire life, and he got overwhelmed."

Morgan stared at his headphones, his laughter subsiding abruptly for real concern. "Are you worried that he might be broken?"

He gave that some thought. If anyone else had asked, his response would have been immediate and angry, but this was his twin. Morgan wouldn't ask if he wasn't truly worried about Slade. If Slade had been broken Morgan would have been among the first to grab the emotional duct tape. "No, I don't think so. He's damaged, yes, but not broken."

"Then love on him as hard as you can." Morgan looked at him and smiled. "He's strong, Magnus. He's had to be. Right now he's dealing with not only the torture but the fact that he's finally free and in a place where it's okay to be weak, where he knows he's safe. Let him get that out any way he has to."

"I will, but I still want to beat the shit out of the Old Man all over again." Magnus would get that chance if the fates were willing. "But for now, I have my marching orders. I'm to protect Sylvia until I can get her home."

Morgan laughed. "Yeah, your mate is one bossy dude."

Magnus grinned, pleased. "Yup, he is."

Morgan shook his head and put the headphones back on. They were in the surveillance van, listening to Sylvia and Sydney chatter at each other. When the women mentioned Frederica's plot against Logan, they exchanged a surprised look.

Magnus's phone rang, startling them. He checked the caller ID, quickly answering when he saw it was Slade. "What's wrong?"

Slade's voice was calm but rough, the raspy tone "I don't know, but I can sense something through the hair bracelet I gave Sylvia. I think she's in danger."

When the lights went out, Magnus was out of the van and rocketing toward the front door of their apartment building, Morgan hot on his heels, his cell phone dropped somewhere in the van. There was no way the lights had gone out in one building on the block. Something was desperately wrong, and Magnus was pulling the plug on their little operation before it had even begun.

He practically ripped the stairway door off its hinges, taking the stairs two at a time. He could barely see in the dim emergency lighting, but that didn't even slow him down. He hauled ass to the third floor, ready to attack anything that made a move on Sylvia.

He opened the third floor door and started running down the dark corridor, but he didn't get very far. There was no emergency light on. Everything was black, the sense that he was not alone nearly overwhelming. He could hear muffled curses, see the flash of lights under doors as the residents attempted to find their way around their suddenly dark apartments. He found himself forced to move slowly, one hand along the wall as he felt for door numbers, praying he found the correct one and didn't accidentally wind up scaring the shit out of some little old grandma with a meat cleaver and a justifiable homicide defense.

A door ahead of him opened and a light flashing into the corridor. He heard Sydney's voice, quiet and grim, shaking slightly. "No one there."

"Good. Let's go." But before the women could leave the apartment Magnus heard a shriek so loud he wouldn't be surprised to find out that Fenris heard it all the way in Rittenhouse Square.

"Sylvia!" Magnus put on a burst of speed as Sylvia's scream rang out. The light moved wildly before the flashlight landed on the carpet, rolling against the wall and pointing in the opposite direction from Magnus, giving him nothing to work with.

Whatever was here was already in the apartment with Sylvia.

Magnus got to the door, terrified he wouldn't be able to stop the attacker from harming his mate. His fingertips sparked in response to his fury. Morgan was right on his heels, muttering under his breath, the thunder building in his voice. Magnus pulled *Mjolnir* from its chain. They wouldn't be able to throw it in the small apartment, but he wanted it ready in case their opponent was more than just a burglar.

The sons of Thor were ready for battle.

Magnus entered first, *Mjolnir* on one hand, lightning sparking from his fingertips.

"Magnus?" Sylvia's trembling voice came from the other side of the room. "Ow!"

He felt the rage build at Sylvia's pain-filled tone. "Morgan."

"On it." Morgan moved around him, edging along the wall, feeling his way toward where Sylvia's voice had come from.

"Well. I wasn't expecting you."

Magnus blinked. That voice was vaguely familiar, feminine yet deep. It was a voice he hadn't heard in decades. "Skadi? Is that you?"

"I hear you've turned traitor, boy." A sense of air displacement was his only warning. Magnus ducked, the blade swishing over his head.

"You still follow the Old Man?" Magnus readied *Mjolnir*, the hammer growing from the tiny silver pendant into the mighty weapon his father had once wielded.

"I follow my lord, the King of the Gods."

Thanks to the light from his fingertips he could just see her. "Then you follow Kir, not Odin." He blocked a blow from Skadi's blade. The strength behind her blow was phenomenal. She wasn't playing around. She intended to kill him if she could. "Kir holds *Gungnir*. He is now the ruler of the gods, not Odin."

"Kir is not my lord." The savage anger in her voice was startling. "He's taken up with the foul betrayer, the Father of Lies."

Apparently she'd had never gotten over the fact that the bonds she'd tied Logan down with had been undone. Kir had freed Logan from his mountain prison, running away with him and hiding out from Odin for centuries.. Since she'd been the one to craft the bonds out of the entrails of one of Logan's sons, she'd been pissed when Logan got away.

But Ragnarrok had begun long before Kir and Logan fled. It started the day Odin tricked the blind god Hodr into nearly killing Kir, but wound up wounding Logan instead. It was only now beginning to come to a head. With the death of Odin, Ragnarrok, the true destiny of the gods, would finally be revealed.

They traded blows, Magnus trying to maneuver Skadi so that Morgan could get the women out to safety. "Why are you here? Why did you attack Sylvia and Sydney?"

"Sylvia and Sydney are nothing more than pawns, a means to get to Loki." Skadi feinted, getting in a solid blow against Magnus's side. He cried out, the pain excruciating. "My orders come from Odin himself."

The fucking bastard was once again using a woman to do his dirty work. First Rina, now Skadi. "Are you his lover now?"

She scoffed. "I have no need for lovers or defenders. I can take care of myself."

The proud daughter of the mountain king had once been married to Njord, the Vanir god of the sea. He felt sorry for the poor guy. She'd given Njord nothing but grief the entire time they'd been married. She'd hated the sea, hated fish, hated sand, but mostly she'd hated her husband and let him know it at every opportunity. Njord had ended the relationship, and ever since then he'd been holed up in the sea, probably thrilled that his ex-wife never visited.

"You're wrong." The sound of *Mjolnir* crashing against her blade was loud and painful enough to distract her from the fact that Morgan had gotten the women out the door. He threw a lightning bolt, making her dance away from the door as Morgan signaled that the hallway was clear. "Kiran Tate-Saeter is the rightful ruler of the Aesir and the Vanir, by the laws of our people and by the prophecy of Ragnarrok."

She swung again, sidestepping his return blow. "You've become weak, almost human. You've lived among them for so long you've forgotten what it is to be jotun."

"I'm half Aesir." Magnus struck with his lightning, pouring his rage into the blow. Skadi flew across the room, her blade falling from her fingers to clatter to the floor. "I am my father's son."

Magnus turned his back on Skadi and walked to the door, but her pain-filled voice stopped him. "This is not the end, Magni Thorsson."

He didn't turn back despite the name he hadn't heard in centuries. "No it is not, Skadi Thjazisdotter." He walked out the door, refusing to run until he'd hit the stairway.

Morgan already had Sylvia and Sydney in the back of the van, the engine running as they waited for Magnus to return. Magnus got into the passenger seat and Morgan took off, the women silent and still behind them.

"You're safe now." He kept repeating that to himself, the visions of what Skadi could have done to Sylvia before he arrived rolling one after the other through his mind. "You're safe."

It was as much reassurance for him as it was for them.

***

When Morgan stepped into the condo, Slade didn't know whether to be relieved or upset. He chose to go with upset when he realized that Morgan was supporting a wounded Magnus. "What happened?" He hurried over, ignoring the lingering twinges of pain, and took Magnus from Morgan. He might be shorter and more slender than Magnus, but he was still a damn horse shifter. He could easily take Magnus's weight.

"Skadi was there." Morgan looked back, and only then did Slade realize that Sylvia and Sydney were with them. Sylvia was limping, her expression pained, her shoes in her hand. "Sylvia twisted her ankle on the stairs when we ran for it."

"What the hell was Skadi doing there? She sticks to her father's country in Jotunheim. I can't remember the last time she came to Midgard." Slade eased Magnus onto the sofa, only then noticing the blood on his lover's side. "She did this?"

Some of his cold fury must have seeped into his tone, because Morgan shot him a startled look. "Yes. She's tough, tougher than I remembered." Morgan helped Sydney settle Sylvia into an armchair near the fireplace, lifting her leg until her ankle rested on the coffee table. It was obviously swollen. "She held Magnus off, but he kept her occupied long enough for me to get Sylvia and Sydney out of the apartment."

So his lover had sacrificed himself for their mate. Slade both approved and disapproved. He grumbled under his breath as he carefully eased the bloody shirt off Magnus. "That cut is deep." Magnus didn't heal the way Slade did. It would take time for the wound to close.

"She told me Odin sent her to deal with Logan." Magnus winced as Slade used the bloody shirt to wipe some of his skin clean. "She's still loyal to him, thinks he should still be the king of the gods."

Slade scowled. "Kir holds Gungnir. He's lord of the Aesir and Vanir now."

"I know that, but the crazy lady doesn't."

Slade made a disgusted noise as he headed into the bathroom for the first-aid kit. He bent down and began rummaging through the cabinets, looking for the red bag Magnus kept under here. He'd become very familiar with that bag since moving in. Magnus broke it out every night, tending Slade's still healing body. Even super jotun healing didn't completely compensate for being skinned alive multiple times in one day. "Great. Wonderful. Now we have to worry about a new player in the game, one who can kick Magnus's ass."

"Hey, now." Slade turned from the bathroom cabinet at the sound of Magnus's voice. "It's okay. I'm okay. I know what she's capable of, and next time I won't hold back."

"You held back?" Slade stood so quickly he almost lost his balance. "Why?"

"The main point was to get Sylvia safely away." Magnus cupped Slade's cheek. "We're all home now, right?"

That touch, coupled with the word home, drained most of Slade's anger. "Yes, we are."

"Now we just have to convince Sylvia of that." Magnus's grin was rueful.

"And Logan, and Kir." Slade rolled his eyes and grabbed the first aid kit. "Go sit. I want to take a look at that wound."

"I've had worse."

"I don't give a shit. Move your ass, Mr. Tate."

Magnus huffed out a laugh. "Yes, dear."

Slade was going to kick the man's ass. Like telling him that Magnus had been hurt far worse made any of it better. He now understood why Magnus growled every time Slade told him about the times Odin had tortured him. He wanted to find Skadi and stomp her into the ground. A few well-placed hooves in her skull would ensure she'd never harm his mates again.

Slade helped Magnus back into the living room, grumbling about the bloody handprints on the wall. Magnus must have used it to prop himself up while he made his way to the master bathroom. Stubborn ass man. He eased Magnus down onto the sofa and immediately opened the first-aid kit. "Morgan, can you get an ice pack for Sylvia's ankle?"

"Already done."

Slade glanced over, nodding his approval at the way Morgan was taking care of Sylvia's swollen ankle. He'd wrapped her ankle in a special brace made to hold ice packs. The fact that Magnus had those ice packs ready to go had him glaring at the man.

Magnus merely smiled at him, seemingly amused by Slade's anger. "It's not the first time one of us has hurt a joint. We have braces for knees, shoulders, the works."

Slade nodded. He supposed he would have to get used to his mate getting hurt. The man was a warrior, a Viking through and through. That didn't mean that Slade wasn't going to give him hell when he came home bleeding, though. "Tell me everything that happened." He glanced at Sylvia, saw the way she was grimacing, holding tightly to Sydney's hand. "Why don't you start?"

She looked startled at his firm tone, but sat up straighter. "We were discussing…" She looked up at Sydney, who shrugged.

"Frederica is planning on planting something on Logan's computer that will break up the relationship between Kir, Logan and Jordan." Magnus was staring at Sylvia grimly. "We were listening."

Sylvia paled. "Then you know we didn't have anything to do with it."

Magnus smiled. "I trust you."

"So do I." Slade taped Magnus up, clucking his tongue when Magnus hissed in pain. "Next time, dodge."

"I did!"

Sylvia, Sydney and Morgan all laughed at Magnus's frustrated yell, but Slade wasn't amused. "Dodge harder."

Magnus rolled his eyes. "Anyway, the lights in the building went out, so Morgan and I knew something was wrong."

"We don't know how, but Skadi managed to get into our apartment without our sensing it." Sylvia picked up where Magnus left off. "The front door and windows didn't open, and it was almost immediately after the lights went out."

"She couldn't have been working alone either. Someone had to cut the power while she made her way into Sylvia's apartment."

"Not necessarily. She might have *Dökk Alfar* blood in her." Slade put away the tape and zipped up the bag. "She could have moved through the shadows to get so quickly from one place to the other. It's the only way."

Dead silence.

"What?" He looked around at the startled faces of every Aesir in the room. "You didn't know that was one of their powers? Odin picked it up centuries ago."

"That explains how he keeps getting away from us." Magnus sounded disgusted. "We—"

The front door slammed open, with Kir, Logan and Jordan storming through. Jordan was the one who spoke, pushing her glasses up her nose as she glared at her brother. "What happened?"

Logan stared at Slade, his relief obvious as he saw that Slade was unharmed. "Fenris smelled blood coming from your apartment and called me."

Magnus grimaced. "We got ambushed by Skadi."

Jordan blinked. "Who?"

Logan cursed, and Kir's eyes began to mist over.

Jordan looked at her husbands and sighed. "I'm going to guess that this is bad."

"Very." Sylvia attempted to stand, but Slade got to her before anyone else. He gently pushed her back into her seat, but her gaze remained on Logan and Kir. "She was sent by Grimm to use Sylvia and I to get to you. She overheard that we were working for you and has declared us traitors, along with anyone following you."

Kir and Logan exchanged a glace as Jordan ran her hand up and down Kir's spine, attempting to soothe him. Jordan was again the one who spoke as the silent communication between Logan and Kir continued. "Who is Skadi?"

"She's an ice jotun whose father was Thjazi, the jotun who kidnapped Idunn. Her father was killed in retaliation, and in compensation she was married off to Kye, but the two couldn't stand each other and wound up divorced."

Kir stared at Logan. "Rumor has it Logan was the one who lured Idunn away from the apple grove."

"I didn't do it!" Logan threw up his hands in frustration. "Every stupid thing that happened back then was blamed on me. The idiot went walking and got kidnapped by a guy who could turn into a giant eagle. Who's to blame? Loki, that's who!" He closed his eyes and took a deep breath as Jordan wrapped her arm around his waist and Kir kissed the side of his neck. "I did some stupid shit back then, but I never deliberately hurt someone. Idunn adores her husband, and he worships her. I never would have endangered either of them."

Sylvia's brows rose as she ran her fingers through her golden hair. "Oh?"

Logan smirked at her. "That was different. Whatever you felt for Thor, it wasn't returned, and you know it." He shrugged. "Besides, you'd pissed me off, remember?"

She blushed. "Oh. That."

"Yeah, that."

"What are you talking about?" Sydney looked between the two, her voice soft and uncertain.

"Nothing." But Sylvia glared at Logan, and Logan's smirk intensified. "It was childish and stupid and cost us both."

The smirk dimmed. "Yeah, it did, didn't it?" Logan sighed. "Truce?"

Sylvia's glared died. "Truce."

"So I rescued Idunn and Thjazi died trying to get her back. But Skadi didn't see it that way and convinced the others that I was the one who'd lured Idunn out of Asgard and allowed Thjazi to make off with her. Since it suited the Old Man to have everyone hating me, he ran with it." Loki took a seat next to Magnus, automatically running his hand over Slade's hair. Slade leaned into the touch, smiling when his father relaxed. "She's been pissed at me ever since. Hell, she's the one who tied me down and put the serpent over me to drip burning poison on me."

"So she's probably thrilled with the idea of killing you." Slade jumped as thunder sounded outside the condo and rain suddenly began to pour from the sky.

"Hey, Blondie. It's all right. We'll get her." Logan held out his hand for Kir, who took it between his own. "Together, right?"

Kir nodded. "All three of us."

"Five, once I spawn." Jordan sighed wearily. "Please, let me spawn soon."

The laughter was a welcome relief.

Chapter Six

"So you two are moving in, all right?"

Sylvia watched as Kir devoured a truly impressive amount of pizza. "We are?"

They'd filled Logan, Kir and Jordan in over a quick dinner of takeout and cola. The only one who even came close to matching him was Slade, who apparently did have the constitution of a horse. From the way Magnus looked at the man, and the way Slade returned those heated glances, it was obvious that not only was that normal but the two of them were together the way Logan and Kir were.

Both Magnus and Slade were delicious, but apparently they were off the menu. Damn it. "Sydney and I will get our own place, right?"

Magnus and Slade both scowled. "You'll move in with us. Sydney will have her own place."

What? "Why would I move in with you two?"

Slade blushed. "I..." He coughed, his voice rough. "I mean, we..." His voice cracked. Slade stared at Magnus. "Mag?"

Magnus's scowl deepened, but there was something there, in his gaze, that made her wonder if just maybe she had a shot at both of them. "Because we said so."

"Here." Kir handed her a key, one with a peanut M&M on it. He handed a completely different one to Sydney. "These are yours."

Sydney was trembling so hard Sylvia was surprised she was still on her feet. "But, we've roomed together for a long time." Syd shot her a terrified look. "Who will remind me to eat?"

Sylvia looked at Slade, then Magnus. "Can she have a key?"

It was Logan who answered. "I don't see why not, until she's got her new roommate anyway." He snickered as Sydney paled. "You'll like her. Trust me."

"Ah. Okay?" Syd practically ran from the room, taking her empty plate and half-eaten slice of pizza into the kitchen.

"She really does forget things like eating and sleeping." Sylvia was worried about her friend. "She won't starve to death, but she'll be miserable and stinky."

Logan seemed shocked. "She wasn't like that when…"

"When you were married?" Sylvia shrugged. "The Internet hadn't been invented back then."

"Is she addicted to online gambling or something?" Kir actually seemed concerned.

"Nope. She found what she's really good at, and she loves it to pieces. Only thing is, she gets caught up in her work and forgets the basics."

"Like combing my hair." Sydney rejoined them, smiling at Sylvia.

"Or peeing."

Sydney giggled. "I hate gravity."

The men looked confused, and Sylvia didn't plan on explaining. She too had gotten caught up in something, realized she was thirsty, and stood, only then to feel the intense need for what Sylvia called a "bio break". Sydney loved her online games, and often used phrases that confused the hell out of Sylvia.

A knock on the door interrupted them, and Logan waved everyone back to their seat. "I'll get it."

He led in Travis and a woman Sylvia didn't know. "Sylvia, Sydney, meet Toni. Toni, this—" he pointed to

Sylvia, "—is Sif, aka Sylvia, and this—" he pointed to Sydney, "—is my ex-wife Sigyn, aka Sydney."

"Hi." Toni waved hello, her dark eyes missing nothing. The woman carried herself like a warrior, like Magnus and Morgan did. She stood with her hands on her hips, surveying the people in the room with the air of someone who was always suspicious, always curious about what people were up to. "Which one of you is Slade?"

Slade held up his hand. "I am."

Toni nodded. "Okay. Let me just—"

"We lied to you." Travis stood with his back to the front door, blocking any possibility of an exit.

Toni did a slow pan toward Travis. Sylvia would have been shaking in her boots, but Travis stood firm in the face of the woman's lowered brow. "Excuse me?"

Logan attempted to placate her. "We have it on good authority that you're in danger."

"Whose authority?" For just a second, Sylvia saw fear flash across Toni's face.

"Nik's."

"That son of a bitch." Toni put out a growl worthy of Fenris. "He's been watching me."

She didn't seem surprised by that. "Why would the Guardian be watching you?" Sylvia didn't understand why Nik would be watching one mortal woman to the point of warning Logan that she was in danger.

Magnus leaned over and whispered in her ear, his breath tickling her. "Toni has Valkyrie blood. She healed Fenris, and Fenris and Logan declared her family. She also helped save Jamie, Jeff's sister, from the Old Man."

"Oh." Yes, that would make her of interest to the Guardian.

"She also doesn't take shit from anyone, not even Kir." Slade seemed in awe of her. "I heard her on the phone with him when he tried to convince her to move in. She's fierce."

"She's also right here." Sylvia glanced over to find Toni glaring at them. "She also has an important job."

"I got you assigned here by your chief." Travis crossed his arms, his missing hand less evident as he did so. "He owed me some favors and I called them in."

Toni's jaw dropped. "Are you fucking *kidding* me? I'm working a homicide right now, I don't have time to babysit your lame ass."

Sylvia laughed. "I think it's more he's babysitting you." When Toni glared, Sylvia laughed harder. "Travis was once lord of the Vanir. He's the strongest warrior we have. If anyone is doing the protecting, it's him."

Travis nodded slowly when Toni stared at him. "I don't know if the danger Nik saw comes from your case or something else, but until he tells me you're safe you'll be living with us."

Kir piped up, holding a key. "With Sydney, to be exact."

Sydney groaned. "Oh, please no. She's going to hate me."

"She won't hate you." Magnus surprised Sylvia by pulling Sydney close and glaring at Toni. "Will she?"

"I might, depending on some things." Toni crossed her arms, not at all intimidated by Magnus's scowl. "For one, was she in on this?"

"No, but I was." Magnus put Sydney behind him and took a step, placing himself before both Slade and Sylvia as well. "And I agree with Nik. There's no way you can defend yourself from the Old Man. Not yet, anyway. He'll tear you apart without a thought. He's killed humans before just to lure us out of hiding, tortured his own grandkids, skinned Sleipnir alive. You think he'll stop at making you uncomfortable?"

"I can take care of myself."

"Against a god?" Magnus's fingertips sparked. "Against someone who can crawl through the shadows to get to you?"

Toni stared at his hands and sighed. "Fine. How long am I in jail for?"

The lightning died from Magnus's fingertips. "It's not jail. It's…family."

She rolled her eyes. "Yeah, yeah. I'm Italian, I know family." She sighed, defeat in her stance and the way the fight went out of her expression. "All right. I get it. And in an odd way, I even appreciate it. I just wish it wasn't necessary. I was this close to capturing a serial killer and now I have to hand the case to someone else."

"I'm sorry about that." Travis exchanged a glance with Magnus and Morgan. "Perhaps we can help to make up for it."

"I'd appreciate that." Toni walked over to Sydney and held out her hand. "I swear to God I'm not a psychopath."

Sydney took Toni's outstretched hand. "I swear I'm not either." She tilted her head. "Unless you count my vampiric assassin dohvakin. She's a freaking nut."

Toni blinked, then her eyes narrowed and an evil smirk crossed her face. "I used to be an adventurer like you."

Syd beamed at Toni. "But then I took—"

"—an arrow to the knee!" The women echoed each other, laughing when they were done.

Sylvia watched as the two women linked arms and began discussing things like armor types, loot, tanking, and melee and ranged fighting styles versus magic. It was as if the rest of them no longer existed. "They're both gonna starve to death."

Magnus shook his head, amused. "Sisters by another mister, huh?"

She huffed out a laugh. "I guess so."

Slade slid between Sylvia and Magnus and put his arms around each of their waists. "I like it."

The wistfulness in his tone had her looking at him sharply. "Slade?"

He surprised her by leaning his forehead against her own. "It's just nice to see family, that's all."

She gazed into his eyes, his pensive expression becoming something more, something warmer. The desire in his gaze caused her pulse to race. His warmth as he stood close seeped into her, his scent filling her senses. Sleek, powerful and beautiful, she could see why Magnus was smitten with him.

He pressed a kiss to her forehead and stepped back, turning to Magnus. "I need to rest." His voice was scratchy, like someone had run a grater over his vocal cords.

"Go. I'll take care of things out here. We'll be in soon."

We?

"Don't do anything that will open up your side." Slade kissed Magnus's cheek. "Good night."

"Good night."

Slade turned toward her. "Don't worry so much. Everything will work out." He pressed another kiss to her forehead. "And get off that foot."

"Yes, Slade."

He smiled sweetly and headed toward what she assumed was the bedroom.

Kir, Logan and Jordan corralled Sydney and Toni toward the front door, Travis not far behind them. "Let's leave these guys alone. We'll show you to your new condo." Travis opened the door. "After you, hothead."

"Thanks, lefty." Logan sauntered out, waving his hand. "Later."

Once they were gone, Sylvia turned to Magnus. "We?"

He frowned for a second before his expression cleared. "Oh. Yes, we." He cupped the back of her head, those strong fingers sliding through her hair. It had been so long since she'd felt a touch like that, a man who wanted her so badly he was trembling with it.

"I thought you and Slade were together."

He slowly smiled. "We are."

But… "Then why are you touching me?"

"Because we want you."

Again with the *we*. She shivered, wondering if it was possible, if what he was saying could possibly be what she was hearing. "Like Logan, Kir and Jordan?"

"Exactly." His fingers tightened, his grip becoming almost painful. "I've wanted you for so long, but I couldn't touch you, not while you still held my father in your heart."

"I don't anymore." Her voice had been reduced to a whisper as she gazed into his moss-green eyes.

"I hoped." His tone was equally quiet. His expression was full of a yearning that hadn't been directed toward her in decades. "Please be ours, Sylvia."

She closed her eyes, her heart at odds with her head. She'd been burnt so badly by his father. Could she offer her heart to another Grimm? Could she take that risk, especially when another fragile heart was involved?

Before she could reply he kissed her, silently begging her to open her mouth and her heart, asking rather than demanding that she submit. It was at total odds with the grip he still had on her head, holding her in place while he slowly, methodically tasted her.

She opened her mouth, getting her first taste of a Grimm man since Thor left her all those years ago. She was shocked at what she discovered.

He tasted right, better than Thor ever had.

The kiss was filled with a longing so intense she trembled, unsure if that yearning need was his or hers.

When he finally lifted his head she had a hard time opening her eyes. She was too busy savoring the things she'd learned from a not-so-simple kiss.

"So. Here's how it's going to be."

That got her to open her eyes. He hadn't let go of her, and the demand was spoken in such a quiet, firm tone she wasn't sure at first if it was an order or not.

"You're going to sleep in the same bed as Slade and I. Nothing, and I mean *nothing*, will happen without your approval. For now, all we'll do is sleep or talk, whatever you prefer." His grip on her head eased. "Slade and I both want you in our lives, but the choice has to be yours."

Sylvia wasn't certain she understood. "Slade barely knows me. Why would he want me?" She'd never been cruel to him when he'd been in his horse form, but she hadn't been all that affectionate either. No one had. They'd been afraid to touch Odin's horse.

"There's more to him than meets the eye. He's been watching all of us for centuries, Sylvia. He probably knows more about how we work than we do. And we're the ones he's chosen, the ones he wants to protect him and love him, whom he wants to protect right back." Magnus smiled. "All either of us wants is a chance." The smile dropped away, and that desperate need was back. "Please."

How could she say no? She had the chance to discover if maybe, just maybe, she'd finally find the one thing she'd been longing for all these years. Slade and Magnus were willing to take a chance on her.

She was more than willing to do the same for them. "Yes."

The relief on his face, the sheer joy, told her this meant more to him that she'd realized. She would do her best not to fuck things up. She wasn't certain how she'd handle two strong-willed men. Could she deal with the fact that the both of them seemed fond of telling her what to do?

Even as Magnus took her to the bedroom she wondered if getting everything she'd wanted would be worth the price.

***

Sylvia woke the next morning knowing two things.

The first thing was, she wasn't alone. Someone was snoring so loudly she was surprised that she'd managed to sleep through it at all.

The second was that she was being watched.

Barely breathing, she opened her eyes, terrified of what she'd find.

A dark gaze held hers. Slade's full lips lifted in a soft smile. "Good morning." His voice was soft, no doubt in consideration of the buzz saw going off behind her.

"Morning." She was still debating the whole *good* thing.

"Sleep well?" He brushed back a strand of her hair, his hand surprisingly calloused. It was one of the many contradictions she'd noticed about Slade Saeter. Soft and hard, sweet yet determined, Slade was a mass of confusing signals.

"Surprisingly, yes, despite Buzz." She hitched her thumb over her shoulder, stifling a laugh as Magnus gave one obnoxiously loud snore.

"We'll get used to it."

"*We* will?" Sylvia was still having a hard time with the change of direction her life had taken.

Slade's expression turned mischievous. "Either that or we smother him in his sleep."

Her eyes crossed. From the decibels coming from Magnus's throat she would have thought he'd gotten the thunder part of Thor's power, not the lightning. "I don't think he'd notice."

Slade's shoulders shook as he tried to stifle his laughter. Those dark eyes were filled with joy as he watched her. "You have no idea how happy I am that you're here." He stroked her cheek, his raspy voice deeper than she'd yet heard it.

Despite Magnus's snoring, there was something intimate about how Slade spoke, the way he cuddled them closer under the sheets. She was wearing a pair of Slade's shorts Magnus had lent her, along with a T-shirt that she was swimming in. She had no doubt her hair was a mess, and her breath would probably cause a dog to barf, but Slade still looked at her as if she was worth more than all the gold in Alfheim. "Then tell me."

She winced. Could she sound any more needy? It had been so long since Sylvia had felt feminine, wanted, that Slade's slowly heating gaze warmed her from the inside out.

"I've watched you for a long time."

Her brows rose. "That's not creepy at all."

He chuckled, the carnal heat morphing into affection. "So I suppose I shouldn't mention how your scent would drive me insane?" He was running his fingers through her hair, gently separating the strands, seemingly fascinated by the texture. "Or how I'd watch you at gatherings, the way your hair shone brighter than the sun. The way you'd try and take care of everyone, or how steadfast you were even when it became obvious Thor wasn't the man you'd hoped he would be."

Thor's memory still hurt, even after all of this time, and it was that memory that kept her from fully embracing the attraction she felt toward Magnus. The man was yummy, his gaze filled with a longing she fully returned, but…

But…

Argh. She was his *stepmother*! How could she get past that?

Magnus and Morgan were the result of an affair Thor had while still married to her, and while she'd resented the mother, she'd done her best not to resent the sons. She hadn't raised them because their mother had, but that didn't mean she couldn't remember a young Magnus running around the *Thing*, the sacred gathering place of the gods, laughing with his twin. Or the teenage Magnus, frowning in concentration as he learned how to fight from his father.

Or an adult Magnus, watching her with a barely hidden hunger she didn't dare acknowledge.

"What's got you frowning, *elskede*?"

Sylvia was startled to hear the endearment from Slade. He couldn't know her well enough to call her his love. "Magnus and Thor."

He nodded. "Does it bother you that you're sleeping with Thor's son?"

"Duh." She glanced over her shoulder, reassured when Magnus didn't wake. She hadn't meant to say that quite so loudly, but at least he'd stopped snoring. "Thor and I were apart for far longer than we were together, but still. I was faithful even when he wasn't."

"Are you worried Magnus will be the same way?" Slade watched her, his expression without judgment. He seemed to understand at least some of her reservations.

"That's part of it. The other part is that he's my stepson."

Slade shook his head. "I could see why that would be an issue, but you didn't raise him. You weren't a mother to him in any sense. It's not as if you were cruel to him, just the opposite. You treated him like the other children of the gods, as if he were just another child of the Aesir. You granted him more courtesy than several of the others did."

It never ceased to amaze her how her fellow Aesir reacted to innocent children. Not all were touted the way

Vali had been, but to her the child was innocent of the father's misdeeds. "How could I do otherwise?"

"Exactly. Magni and Modi were raised by their jotun mother, not you, but you still treated them the way I would have wanted to be treated." Slade wrapped one of her curls around his finger. "I think no one could fault you for the attraction as they might if you *had* raised him."

There was something about Slade that allowed her to speak her deepest fear. The fact that he spoke as if her worries were valid helped a great deal in making her trust him. "I don't know if I fear the judgment of others or myself."

"That's something you'll have to figure out on your own. I can say that your own judgment is far more important, but unless you believe it I could say it until the moon turns purple and it won't have any real effect." The whole time they spoke he continued to play with her hair. "If it helps, Magnus and I have both longed for you for centuries. We've both watched while you broke your heart over Thor, and when he left you I'm certain Magnus cheered just as loudly as I did. And while I never thought I'd get the chance to touch you like this, Magnus always dreamed, always hoped, so I hoped it for him too."

He was going to break her heart. "Because you never thought you'd get away from Odin."

"I thought he'd finally kill me before he let me go free, yes." Slade smiled softly. "But Magnus saved me. He'll save you too if you let him."

"Can we be saved?" Sylvia bit her lip, still uncertain that everything was going to wind up the way Slade obviously hoped they would.

"I think so." He lifted a strand of her hair to his lips. "We're willing to wait a bit longer while you decide if this—" he let go of her hair long enough to gesture between the three of them, "—is something you can live with. And if you're truly worried about the others, all you have to do is ask them. Not one of them seemed upset by the fact that Magnus and I claimed you as ours."

"You did?" She blinked, uncertain if she'd been there or not. She hadn't had her coffee yet, so her brain wasn't completely awake. Yet another thing that seemed to make confiding in Slade so easy. "And no one thought anything of it?"

"Nope." He chuckled softly. "And I've learned with this bunch that they aren't afraid to make their opinions known." He widened his eyes comically.

She laughed. "Good point."

"So." He cupped her chin. "Can I kiss you good morning now?"

Her breath caught at the sweet desire in his gaze. "Yes. Please."

His smile was sheer beauty, but she didn't get to see it for long. Slade swept his lips over hers, gently at first, but growing increasingly more demanding. She parted her lips, eager to get her first taste of him, to see if he was just as delicious as Magnus.

He was, in his own unique way. Where Magnus had been as fiery as his hair, Slade was all about slowly building on what had started as a simple sweetness. He took his time, forcing her to acknowledge that the growing heat between them wasn't all on his side. The slow burn that began to build had her curling closer to him, eager for his touch, for the feel of sleek, masculine skin. She wanted more, deeper, sweeter, hotter, but Slade insisted on keeping it—

They broke apart as Magnus snored so loudly he startled himself awake. "Huh? Wha?" Sylvia rolled onto her back to see Magnus staring at them blearily. "Oh. Hi."

Slade started to laugh, leaning his head against her shoulder.

"What's so funny?" Magnus looked adorably confused, an expression she'd never once seen on his father's face. Then again, Magnus was turning out to be nothing like Fred Grimm, and for that she was beginning to be grateful rather than afraid.

"You are." She reached out and stroked the stubble on his cheek. "But that's okay. We like you that way."

Slade laughed harder.

"If you say so." Magnus shook his head at them, but he was watching them with such joy it was obvious he was just happy they were there.

She patted his chest. "We do, Buzz."

He cocked an eyebrow. "Buzz?"

Sylvia smiled and wiggled out of bed, crawling from in between them by sliding over Slade. "I've got dibs on the bathroom!"

Both men were staring at her as she ran for it, Magnus still looking adorably confused and Slade with a return of the sweet heat that had been building between them. She was slamming the door shut when she finally heard them jump from the bed.

"So not fair," she heard Magnus complain. "How come she climbs on you and not me?"

Sylvia stifled her giggles as she went about her business. It looked like living with the two men would never be boring.

Chapter Seven

"Calm down, Slade. Deep breaths."

Slade did as told, Magnus's arm around him, supporting him. He leaned into Sylvia's touch as she caressed his forehead.

"What's wrong? Why are you so pale?" Her concern touched him. When he'd woken that morning she'd been sleeping peacefully, one hand on his chest, her face serene. Her backside had been pressed up against Magnus, the big man curled around her protectively.

Slade had almost cried, he'd been so happy. When they'd spoken, and she'd opened up to him, he'd been ecstatic. The kiss they'd shared had been amazing, all golden light and sweet, sweet heat. He'd thought he was dreaming until Magnus snored so loudly he woke himself up, causing Slade to break into laughter. Magnus had been confused, Sylvia amused, and Slade had completely forgotten about seeing Fenris this morning.

Fenris, who would be at Logan's along with the rest of the family, waiting for them.

Waiting for him.

Slade didn't know if Jeff had warned his mate that Slade was coming, let alone that he wanted to speak to him. Fenris's cool attitude wasn't inspiring any confidence in Slade, despite Jeff's words of support. "Family."

"Oh." Sylvia hugged him, startling him. "It'll be all right, Slade."

"She's right." Magnus pressed a kiss to his forehead as Slade hugged Sylvia back, enjoying her softness as much as he'd loved Magnus's hard body snuggled against his. "And if it's not we'll take you home, I swear."

Home. His knees went weak just thinking of it. He had a *home*. Everything else was just icing on the cake. "All right. I can do this." He squared his shoulders and took hold of their hands, one on either side of him. "Besides, if worse comes to worst I already know I'm faster than Fen."

Sylvia laughed, the joyful sound making him smile back.

Magnus, on the other hand, just rolled his eyes. "C'mon, ya big chicken. Let's go eat pancakes."

"Bwok." Slade clucked, making Sylvia laugh harder.

Magnus just shook his head and dragged them through Logan's front door. "Hey, we're here."

Slade stared around the room and smiled. Everyone was there. Logan, Kir and Jordan were laying out the food. Jamie sat next to Travis, her hand on his shoulder as she leaned in close. Val was trying to get Sydney's attention, but she was hiding behind Toni, who kept trying to dodge out of the way so Val could get to her. It looked like a weird dance they were performing.

Jeff and Fenris were cuddled together on the couch, staring at Slade, Magnus and Sylvia.

Slade nodded toward them, wondering if this was where things went to hell or not. "Brother."

Fenris closed his eyes and shuddered. "Brother." He stood, holding Jeff's hand so tightly his knuckles were white. "How are you?"

"I'm good." Slade glanced at Jeff, who was nodding encouragingly. "And you?"

"I'm—" Fenris gulped. He let go of Jeff's hand and held out his arms. "Please?"

Magnus gently pushed Slade forward. "Go on."

Like Slade wasn't going to embrace his brother. The pain in Fenris's gaze was killing him. Slade ran toward Fenris, catapulting into his arms.

Fenris caught him easily, the deep, shuddering sigh that rocked him exposing his true feelings. Jeff had been right. Fenris truly had wanted to accept him, but Slade's injuries had kept him back.

"It's okay." He found himself in the odd position of soothing the beast. Fenris was shaking, his embrace becoming so tight it was almost painful.

"No, it's not, but it will be." Fenris finally shook himself and let Slade go. "Welcome home, little brother."

Slade grinned. "Thanks."

Fenris nodded once, then stepped back. He took hold of Slade's arm and guided him away from the others. Once far enough apart, he pushed back the sleeve of Slade's long-sleeved T-shirt, growling at the marks on his skin. "Tell me who is to kill Odin." His voice was low, barely audible. "You said in one of your phone calls that he was closer to us than we thought."

"I think the one who will do it is our brother." Slade glanced around, keeping his voice as soft as Fenris's.

Fenris gaped at him before quickly glancing around and leaning in close. "Jörmungandr?"

"No, Nari."

"What? But…he's dead."

"No, he's not. He's been in hiding all these years." Slade stepped closer and lowered his voice even more, praying no one but Fenris heard him. "Think about it. It's the only thing that makes sense.

O'er the sea from the north there sails a ship
With the people of Hel, at the helm stands Loki;
After the wolf do wild men follow,
And with them the brother of Byleist goes.

"You tried to kill Odin and failed. What other wolves of Loki's line are there?"

Fenris's eyes went wide. "By the gods, I think you're right. *That's* the other werewolf." Fenris was staring at Logan, who was smiling at them both, obviously pleased the brothers were chatting. He smiled, but Slade could see the effort it took to do so. "This will kill Pappa."

Slade agreed. Vali was supposed to kill the wolf that killed Odin in retaliation, but Slade was certain it wasn't going to go down quite the way they all thought it would. "I'm almost positive I am. All the clues, once you dismiss you as the wolf, point toward Nari. The good news is I don't think Odin has figured it out yet." And Slade hadn't dared say it with Hugin and Munin, Odin's little spy ravens, watching his every move. He'd hoped his father would have figured it out from the clues he had given them, but it seemed none of them had.

"But you did." Fenris slapped him on the back, staggering him. "Now all we need to do is find him and bring him home."

"It won't be that easy. Nari was driven mad by the transformation and it's only gotten worse over the centuries. He's not human any longer, not in any sense of the word." In fact, Slade was almost positive that Nari had been Jack the Ripper, tearing into his victims with a cold viciousness that fascinated the world to this day. "He's become the monster everyone believed you were."

Fenris swore softly in multiple languages. Slade was impressed. He only understood half of what his brother said, but it was inventive. "Have you seen him?"

Slade nodded. "From afar, yes. I didn't dare get closer." And what he'd seen had sent cold chills down his spine. When Loki had been bound to the mountain, his sons Nari and Narfi had been taken there as well. To punish Loki, he'd transformed Nari into a wolf. Maddened by it, Nari had shredded Narfi and disappeared. Narfi's entrails had been turned into Loki's bindings. "I wish I could tell you he'll be able to join us when this is all over, but he's a psycho. I wouldn't want him anywhere near Magnus and Sylvia."

"I can understand that." Fenris glanced at Jeff before turning his attention once more to Slade. "Did Skye do this?"

Slade tilted his head, confused. "By changing the prophecy?" When Fenris nodded glumly, Slade smiled. "No. That happened after Nari was changed. I think she just saw a way to save you and took it."

"Are you sure?" Fen glanced at Morgan. "It will hurt him a great deal, and her as well, if they discover Skuld drove Logan's son insane."

"I'm positive." The prophecy of Ragnarrok had already been written, but the *meaning* of it had not been fully revealed. It would not be until things came to pass. Only the Norns of Fate knew the how, the why and the where.

"The thing is I don't know where he is right now. Odin seems to have forgotten about him completely because he's convinced you're the one who will kill him. The others barely remember him." Except for Sydney, who watched the very pregnant Jordan with a wistful, pained expression she was quick to hide whenever anyone glanced her way. She, like Logan, knew the pain of losing her children.

"Except you." Slade leaned into Fenris's embrace. "My smart brother."

Slade chuckled. "Yeah. So smart I stayed under the thumb of a madman for centuries."

"You avoided my fate."

"He tortured us both, Fen."

"And he'll pay for that, I swear it." Logan's voice interrupted their bonding time, but Slade didn't mind. His father's arms came around them both. "I heard what you said," he whispered. "So did Kir. We'll look into it."

Slade looked into his father's eyes and saw the grief that never quite went away. "I'm sorry."

"Me too." Logan ruffled his hair. "You have no idea how proud I am of you, but you'll learn." He winked. "In the meantime, there's someone else who'd like to see you."

Slade tilted his head. Everyone was already here. "Who?"

Logan waved his hand and, to Slade's surprise, a portal opened. "How?"

"Death can go wherever she chooses, through any barrier." Logan's pride shown through as Hel and Hodr stepped through.

"Holy shit." Hel. Hel was here. Slade hadn't hoped to meet his sister for quite some time, not until closer to Odin's demise. "Hel."

The beautiful woman with the black hair and ice-blue eyes smiled. "Sleipnir, Fenris. You have no idea how much I've wanted to see you two. Hodr told me I should just make the time, so when Pappa called and invited us to breakfast we jumped at the chance." She glided forward, leaving Hodr at the closing portal. "Give your big sister a kiss!"

While Fenris, Logan and Slade greeted Hel, Kir and Jordan were busy hugging Hodr. "That condo I saved for you is still available, sweetheart," Kir called over to Hel. "Any time you want it, you and Hodr can stay. It's under the name Holden and Helen Tate."

Hodr smiled and tilted his head. "That's very nice of you, Kir, but Hel has been pretty busy down below." The blind god tilted his head toward Hel, his expression loving. "I'm going to try and get her to visit more often, though."

"Now that my brothers are coming home I think we'll see if we can make the time, dear." Hel put one arm around Slade and the other around Fenris. "So. Introduce me to your mates."

Hel had inherited their father's evil, mischievous grin. The goddess of Death, ruler of Helheim and daughter of the Trickster, seemed right at home in Logan, Jordan and Kir's condo.

Sylvia stepped forward, holding her hand out to Hel. "It's good to see you again, Hel."

Hel's eyes gleamed with amusement. "And you, Sylvia."

Magnus and Jeff stepped forward, and before Slade knew it he was surrounded by family.

With just a few more touches his dream would finally be realized. Nothing would take what he'd gained today away from him.

***

"Hide me."

Magnus held still while Sydney ducked behind him. She was quivering with fear, her eyes huge as she peeked out from behind his back. Sylvia and Syd had been with them for a week, and Syd was turning out to be a lot more squirrely than he remembered. Every single time they came to Logan, Kir and Jordan's for breakfast Syd hid behind someone as soon as she saw Val. Today it seemed to be his turn. "Um. Syd? What's going on?"

"He's here." She pointed with a shaking finger toward Val.

"And?" He turned to face her, surprised to see her cheeks were flushed. "You know he won't hurt you, right?"

"But he's just so…" Her hands fluttered wide. "And he's so…" They fluttered again, this time way over her head. "Plus he's kind of…" She fanned her red face. "So I'm hiding."

Magnus stared at her, wondering what the fuck was going on. He was pretty sure she was having some sort of seizure. "Maybe we should get Kir to take a look at you."

Syd huffed in frustration before resting her head against his chest. "I don't want to get blown up, or chopped up, or skewered." She tilted her head with an adorable frown. "Maybe skewered. Depending."

She was totally confusing the fuck out of him. He needed backup, and he needed it now. "Sylvia!"

"You bellowed?" Sylvia was suddenly there, staring at Sydney with the same confused expression he was pretty sure was on his own face. "What's Syd doing?"

"Spazzing."

Syd's hands flew all over the place before settling on his chest. She never once lifted her head from him. "Val," she whispered in the most embarrassed tone he'd ever heard.

"Ah." Sylvia glanced behind him toward the Avenger, biting her lip. Her confused expression had cleared. "C'mon, Syd. I can use some help baking cookies."

Syd's head slowly lifted off her chest. "You want to poison him?"

Magnus choked out a laugh before he could stifle it.

From the glare Sylvia shot him she'd heard it. "I'm not that bad a cook."

Syd stared at her, her jaw hanging open.

Magnus just turned his back to them both, terrified his soon-to-be lover would see his fight to control his laughter. She might decide to get even with him by making him something to eat. Sylvia had the urge to take care of everyone around her, and for the most part she did a wonderful job. But if he had any say in it, she'd be banned from the kitchen for eternity. She was an absolute disaster where food prep was involved. It was a good thing he had several food delivery places on speed dial, or he would have starved long ago. Not even Logan could take something Sylvia had cooked and make it edible, and the man could be considered a master chef.

Apparently Syd was braver than he was because she had no trouble teasing Sylvia. "I'm just saying, it's a good thing Slade can eat hay."

"Hmph." Sylvia's tone was disgusted. "See if I ever make you mango pudding again."

He turned just as Syd did a triumphant fist pump. Unable to hold back his laughter, he tried to grab hold of Sylvia, only laughing harder when she started to smack his arm. "Sweetheart, I think it's safe to say your talents lie outside the kitchen."

She snarled like a cute little kitten.

He kissed the tip of her nose. "Aw, sweetie. You're so cute when you're trying to be mean."

She huffed and puffed, but eventually she settled down against him. "I hate you all."

"Mm-hm." Magnus was far too busy enjoying the feel of her in his arms to argue with her. He settled his cheek against the top of her head and closed his eyes, humming happily under his breath.

"You suck."

"Mm-hm." He rocked her back and forth, swaying gently in time with the music of their heartbeats.

She sighed deeply and relaxed in his arms. "Damn it."

He chuckled. "You sound so disgusted with yourself."

"I caved like a spineless jellyfish, all because you hummed."

So instead of the tuneless nothing he'd been doing he started humming "The Gummy Bear Song".

She didn't react at all in the way he'd expected. She pulled free and, instead of laughing (or beating on him), she took one look at Syd and started singing.

The two women danced around each other, head banging when they sang the *beba bi duba duba yum yum* part of the song until he was laughing so hard he was clutching his sides. They looked utterly ridiculous, dancing some strange Snoopy dance and flopping around like idiots.

He'd never seen Sylvia like this, playing and being silly and just loving life. She was flushed, smiling and laughing, at ease in her own skin despite the fact that she looked like she had some weird floppy head disorder. When she Muppet-flailed he finally understood what women meant when they said they would die from cuteness overload.

She was absolutely adorable and having the time of her life. He needed to make sure she got more moments like these, where she felt comfortable enough to just let go and let her inner geek out to play.

"What the fuck did you do to them?" Slade was next to him, watching the antics of the two women with a bemused, utterly charmed smile. "You finally broke them, didn't you?"

"That's one of the most annoying songs in the universe. I think I like it." Logan was watching from the kitchen doorway, a huge grin on his face. Jordan was tucked against him, holding her stomach as she, too, lost herself in laughter. Kir was right behind them both, his head tucked against Logan's neck, one hand on each of their shoulders.

Val merely stood, his gaze glued to Syd, looking utterly gobsmacked. A slow, hungry smile crossed his face as Syd gyrated like a woman covered in itching powder. Magnus didn't even know arms could bend like that without breaking, but Syd must be part Gumby.

When they finished their song Magnus and Slade both clapped, the rest of the family soon doing the same. Sylvia bowed, but Syd curtsied, each woman flushed and happy.

Sylvia threw herself into his arms, grinning widely, just so pleased with herself she was read to burst.

Syd looked just as happy until she caught sight of Val watching her and hid once more behind Magnus. "Eep."

The scowl Val suddenly sported wasn't helping his cause. He threw his hands up in disgust. "I didn't do anything!"

Syd shook so hard Magnus was afraid she'd hurt herself.

Val sighed wearily. "I'll go eat breakfast at my place."

"Uncle Val, please don't." Jordan held out her hand to him, distressed.

Val shook his head. "I tell you what. I'll come back, all right?" He sounded almost depressed. "Syd, I swear I won't hurt you."

There was the ring of magic in his words, a vow he was now bound to, but Syd didn't move. She merely nodded, but she was tucked so far behind Magnus he wasn't sure if Val could see it or not.

"Okay?" Val sounded unsure, so perhaps he hadn't seen Syd's assent.

"Okay," she muttered.

Val started to leave, but froze when Syd spoke softly once more. "Stay."

He glanced at her, but she refused to look back. "Okay."

She nodded against Magnus's back once more and then moved away. She sat as far from Val as she could get, refusing to look at him.

As everyone else settled at the table Val respected the distance she'd put between them by staying away from her for the rest of the meal, but he watched her like a hawk. When the only thing she put on her plate was some fruit he saw Val lean over and whisper something in Kir's ear that had the man getting up to put some pancakes on her plate, much to her surprise.

"You're way too thin, Syd." Kir smiled sweetly and ruffled her hair. "We need to fatten you up."

Syd rolled her eyes, but her expression was pleased as she poured syrup over her pancakes. Val waited until she looked down again before nodding his thanks to Kir.

Val had decided to take care of Syd, whether she knew it or not. Magnus was aware of how patient his uncle could be when he wanted something.

And it was more than obvious that Val wanted Syd.

He leaned over and whispered in Sylvia's ear. "Does Val have a shot?"

"Hmm?" She glanced up from the meal Logan was placing at the table. "Pfft. Oh hell yes. She's been crushing on him for years."

"Years?" Magnus's brows rose.

"Yeah, but she's scared too." Sylvia's gaze darted toward Logan, and Magnus understood. "Val is big, scary and could break not only her heart but the rest of her as well."

"And her heart's already been broken once."

"Mm-hm. Val's vow will help, but she's still scared of her shadow. She's terrified the Old Man will get hold of her and mess with her mind again, make her question who and what she is."

Magnus frowned. "He fucked with her?"

"Big time. She was Logan's ex, the one who knew him best, remember? Of *course* he went after her, more than once."

"Son of a bitch." Magnus sat back and stared at Syd, a lot of things about her now clear to him. "Did he use Val?"

"No, but I think the threat of Val was more than enough."

"I really need to kick the Old Man's ass again." Odin needed to pay big time for the lives he'd nearly destroyed.

Sylvia patted his hand. "You'll get the chance, I'm sure of it. In the meantime, pass the pancakes."

"Yes, dear."

"Remember that phrase. Practice it. You'll be saying it a lot." She grinned and took the plate from him.

He grinned right back, happy as a pig in mud. "Yes, dear."

Chapter Eight

"Have you found anything yet?" Magnus was watching Sydney work, fascinated by the way she got so lost in her computer that nothing else seemed to matter. In fact, one of the reasons he was in the room with her was to ensure she ate. Whenever meal time came up one of them would bring her food and hover around until she finished it. Even Toni had discovered that Sydney was a hound dog on a scent when it came to chasing a lead on the computer. She'd also taken to watching out for Sydney.

It was good to see the concern Toni had for her new roommate. While they still had some things to work out, Toni and Sydney looked like they were going to do just fine as roommates. As for the rest of them, Sydney was slowly starting to open up to them. The only one who couldn't get close to Sydney at all was Val. Sydney seemed terrified of him, and it was driving the big guy crazy. He couldn't understand why she was so afraid of him when she merely seemed shy with everyone else.

"I've been through everything on here, and there's nothing I can find that would lead to the break-up of Logan and Kir." She ran her fingers through her hair, frustrated beyond belief. "I'm beginning to think I'll never figure this out."

Magnus knew how she felt. Sylvia had opened up to Slade and Magnus, but she had yet to initiate any of the touches or kisses she seemed to relish so much. She was holding back, driving them insane with her shy glances and soft smiles. She slept in the same bed as them, but it was still more like she was humoring them than she actually wanted to be there.

If not for Slade, Magnus would have lost his damn mind by now. Slade kept his temper even. He refused to give in to the impatience Magnus felt so keenly, believing they simply needed to give Sylvia time to realize what he already knew, that the three of them belonged together.

Slade's certainty didn't quite banish Magnus's fears that somehow he'd lose Sylvia. He'd waited too long, wanted too desperately to eliminate those fears completely. Not until Sylvia gave in would he be able to release the anxiety that dogged him day in and day out.

"How's it going in here?"

Magnus started, unaware that Logan had slipped into the room. "Damn it, hothead. Don't scare me like that unless you want a hammer to the face."

Logan grinned. "Aw, did I scare you?"

There was the Trickster Magnus remembered, delighting in making those around him uncomfortable.

No. That wasn't quite right, and Magnus could see that now. Logan simply enjoyed having fun, but things had been so tense under Odin's rule that Loki's tricks had been seen as malicious rather than a cry for help. So instead of barking at Logan for making him jump, Magnus merely rolled his eyes. "Bite me."

Logan shuddered. "That is wrong on so many levels." He put his hand on Magnus's shoulder. "And call me Pappa."

Magnus gagged.

Logan snickered.

Magnus decided to address the one thing he knew would focus Logan's attention. "Slade's feeling much better."

The relief on Logan's face made Magnus glad he'd said something. "So he's not hiding anything from me?"

Well. Magnus hadn't expected that to be one of Logan's worries. "No, he's not. He really is doing better, at least physically. The nightmares are still there, but he knows he's safe. Hopefully with enough time they'll ease."

Logan's expression turned haunted. "Not entirely." He took a deep breath, and his features eased. "But you and Sylvia will help with that."

Magnus hoped so. If anyone knew about the end result of long-time torture it was Logan. "I'll do everything in my power to help him, and I think Sylvia feels the same way." She'd held Slade, too, soothing him when he woke crying in the night. That Slade hadn't broken under Odin still amazed Magnus. "Your son is so strong, Logan. I'm in awe of him." Magnus hated to admit it, but if he'd gone through what Slade had he wasn't certain he would be as whole as his mate.

Logan bit his lip. "I just wish he hadn't needed to be."

Magnus wished the same thing, but the past couldn't be changed. They had to deal with the hand life had given them.

"I actually slipped in here to tell you that Skadi's been testing the wards."

Damn it. Magnus had hoped she'd give up, but he should have known better. Skadi had stuck with Njord as long as she had out of sheer stubbornness. "Any chance of her breaking through?" Magnus laughed at the look of disgust on Logan's face. "All right then. She's got jotun magic like you, so I was worried for a sec."

"It better have been only a second. I can run rings around Skadi in my sleep."

"Shh, I'm trying to work here." Sydney glared at them both over her shoulder before turning back to Logan's monitor.

Logan made exaggerated shushing motions as he tiptoed out of the room. He chuckled as he closed the door. "It's nice to see she's grown a spine."

"I didn't know she could growl like that." Magnus was grinning as he saw Jeff showing Slade how to play on the Wii. Sylvia had one of the controllers and was surprisingly good, swinging it around like a sword. She whooped as she decapitated a bad guy. "Remind me not to piss her off."

"Which one?" Logan was smiling as well. Slade was laughing, holding his sides as Jeff high-fived Sylvia. Fenris was sitting behind his mate, quietly watching, always guarding him. The simple joy on his face was almost painful to see. "Two out of four."

Magnus blinked, the significance of that not hitting him until he really looked. "Hel is happy, Logan. Hodr takes almost as good care of her as Kir does of you. And we'll bring Jörmungandr home too."

Logan nodded absently. "Someday I'd like to see all of them together, when it's safe."

"Maybe you can take them to Disney World, Pappa."

Logan flipped him the bird.

"What are you two up to?" Sylvia was still grinning, flush with her triumph over a pixilated Sith. It was a good look for her, one he hoped to see more often.

There was no way he was going to tell her about Skadi, not now. The last thing he wanted was to cause either Slade or Sylvia to worry. Logan would make sure the wards were secure, with help from Jordan. So he took hold of her hand and tugged her into his arms, aware Jeff had paused the game. He widened his eyes, trying to look as innocent as possible. "What makes you think we're up to something?"

Her gaze narrowed. "Magnus."

Her amused warning tone, the way her hands gripped him, kept him close, made him shudder with need. "You having fun, sweetheart?"

Sylvia's cheeks flushed and she turned her eyes away, trying to hide the desire he'd glimpsed. "I'm kicking ass." She suddenly laughed, looking back up at him, no longer hiding the growing affection he could sense for everyone. She leaned in closer, and her scent enveloped him, warm jasmine and woman. "Slade sucks at this game."

"I do not." Slade's indignant tone made her giggle.

"He so does. He keeps knocking Jeff's character off of cliffs."

Slade crossed his arms over his chest. "I did that on purpose."

"Sure you did," Sylvia drawled, but as soon as Slade turned away from them she shook her head, making Magnus stifle a laugh.

"I saw that, you traitor." Slade was glaring at them both equally, so Magnus wasn't sure which one of them he was speaking to. His pale, shoulder-length hair was mussed, as if he'd been running his fingers through it repeatedly. The dark T-shirt Jeff had given him was oddly appropriate for the game they were playing. Slade had laughed when he'd seen Darth Vader's head replaced with that of a horse with the words *May the Horse Be With You*. His jeans hugged his thighs, showcasing his lean strength.

In contrast, Sylvia was in a casual, breezy blue-and-white maxi dress with short sleeves. Pale gold sandals adorned her feet, her painted toes peeping out from under the hem. Her hair was pulled back into a long ponytail, and she'd chosen to go with minimal makeup. It was the most casual he'd ever seen her, and it delighted him. She'd dressed for a day at home, surrounded by friends and family. It was wonderful to see this relaxed side of her, and he made a mental note to thank Jeff for putting that beautiful smile on her face.

"Get back here so I can kick your ass." Slade was giving Sylvia the most evil grin imaginable. "And this time we're playing Mario Kart."

This time it was Magnus who had to hold his sides as he laughed.

***

Sylvia wanted to scream, she was so confused. On the one hand, living with Magnus and Slade was surprisingly easy. Both men made a point of including her in everything that went on. When Slade had a nightmare, he turned toward her just as often as he did Magnus. When Magnus was upset over their lack of progress in stopping Frederica or Odin, he showed it to both Sylvia and Slade equally, expecting them to be able to handle everything he threw at them as if it were the most natural thing in the world.

When Sylvia lost her temper over the fact that neither man knew how to hang up a wet towel both men apologized and promised to do better. And they did, surprising her even further when they asked what she wanted changed around the condo. Slade went so far as to break out a laptop and show both Magnus and Sylvia what he liked and making notes on their comments. Their tastes didn't quite mesh perfectly, but Sylvia could see how they could take Magnus's condo and make it theirs instead of his. Magnus was all for that, voicing his opinion when he felt Sylvia's choices might be too feminine, or arguing about keeping his couch but compromising on the side chairs she fell in love with at first sight.

It wasn't perfect, but she hadn't expected it to be. What it was scared the hell out of her.

It was *real*. They fought, they laughed, they spent quiet time just reading, and all the while they let her know that she was part of them in subtle ways she couldn't deny.

They touched constantly, both her and each other. Slade would lie with his head on Magnus's lap while they talked quietly, perfectly at ease while Sylvia read. Magnus would stroke her hair in passing, tugging on the strands to get her attention. Slade would slip her a glass of whatever he was drinking, silently taking care of her. When it came to video games she was just as ruthless as they were, making both men pout when she beat their asses or pouting herself when they beat hers.

It was both simple and profound, the way she'd so easily slipped into their lives. And true to their word, they did no more than kiss. But the best times were when all three of them were tangled together in front of the television, watching whatever movie whoever had won rock-paper-scissors had put on. Relaxed, they'd chat quietly, laugh, and simply enjoy each other's company.

Never in all her years had she felt so deeply that she belonged right where she was, not even when she'd first moved in with Sydney, both of them frightened at being on their own. She found herself laughing more, sighing more, even snarling more than she had in…

Forever.

And it was all because the two men who'd invaded her life had allowed her to invade theirs in return.

She felt a soft tug on her hair and knew instantly it was Magnus. "What are you thinking about so deeply?"

She glanced up at him, taking her eyes off the television show she hadn't even been watching. "You two, what else?"

"Are you getting over the fact that I'm Thor's son?" He settled on the sofa next to her, watching her with a troubled gaze.

Slade must have told him what they'd spoken about while he slept. Two weeks ago she might have been upset, but seeing the way the two of them meshed she wasn't surprised that Magnus knew what Slade did. It was just another part of their charm. "I'm working on it." It was turning out to be easier than she'd thought it would be too. The fact that he was nothing like his father helped a great deal.

"Good." He grinned, his relief obvious. He held out his hand to Slade, who joined him on the sofa. "In that case, we'd like to try something."

She stared at them suspiciously. "If this involves those aquavit Jell-O shots you were trying to talk me into, the answer is still no."

Slade slowly smiled. "I still think we could have fun with those."

"No, Slade." For someone who'd been stuck in Asgard for most of his life he certainly had a unique grasp of modern culture. "I'm not doing it."

He reached out and placed his hand on her knee, rubbing her skin through the thin cotton of her sundress. "I'll persuade you. Eventually."

That grin on Slade's face was lethal. Magnus had an equally naughty look. She sat back, feeling remarkably like a doe during mating season. "Now I know you two are up to something."

They looked at each other, and a tingle of anticipation had her shuddering. She was starting to get an idea of what they wanted, and she couldn't say she was averse to the idea. She just wasn't sure the timing was right. At least Slade was fully healed now, even if he was scarred. And Magnus had made his desires more than clear while respecting her need for time.

She licked her lips, already anticipating the taste of them, hot and sweet like the best candy. Chocolate with peppermint, sweet with a bite to it, was her all-time favorite. She got that with the two of them.

Slade must have seen her decision, because he held out her hand. "Nothing you don't want, remember?"

Magnus echoed his lover, holding out his hand for her as well. "We'll go slow, even if it kills me."

Slade rolled his eyes, and Sylvia laughed. "You've been a good boy so far, Magnus. Keep up the good work and we'll give you a cookie."

Magnus grunted. "I just want to be the filling in the cookie sandwich."

Slade blinked, his cheeks turning bright red. "Really?"

"Really." Magnus kissed Slade, but Slade appeared too stunned to return it. Now Magnus's cheeks were pink. "I like it both ways."

Slade's eyes went wide, and suddenly Sylvia found herself yanked to her feet along with Magnus. Slade was a *lot* stronger than he seemed. "Let's go."

Magnus was laughing as Slade dragged them into the bedroom. "Whoa there."

Slade glared at him. "Did you just *whoa* me?"

Now Sylvia was giggling.

"You did not just whoa me," Slade muttered, yanking Magnus's shirt over his head.

"Yes, he did." Sylvia laughed harder as Slade pushed Magnus down onto the bed.

"You are so going to pay for that." Slade tugged Magnus's pants off while Magnus watched indulgently.

"Yes, dear. Whatever you say, dear." Magnus hissed as Slade licked the head of his cock. "Just as long as you keep doing that, dear."

Sylvia watched as Slade, still mostly dressed, eased Magnus's underwear down so that Magnus's cock was fully exposed. He grabbed the sides of Slade's head and held him steady as he fed his cock to Slade. Sylvia moaned at the sight of Magnus's length disappearing between Slade's lips.

Magnus, his expression dazed, looked at her and frowned. "Do you want to get naked?"

With an audible slurp Slade lifted his mouth off of Magnus. "Only what she wants, remember? If all she does is watch that's fine by me."

"Me too, but I thought she might want to touch."

She hadn't heard such a falsely innocent tone since the last time Logan tried to lie to her. "Mm-hm." But she found herself pulling off her sundress anyway, smiling when Slade went back to driving Magnus insane.

Magnus held out his hand to her. "Your choice, sweetheart."

Slade continued with his self-appointed task, but the glance he shot her was full of need.

Sylvia took the final step, and grasped Magnus's hand.

Chapter Nine

"C'mere." Magnus pulled Sylvia down onto the bed and helped her remove the rest of her clothes. The flimsy panties and lacy bra were carefully draped over the end of the bed, and Slade got his first look at Sylvia in all her glory.

She was magnificent, all gold and peach and perfectly shaped. Slade took his mouth off of Magnus's cock and stared at her before moaning and taking one of her ripe nipples into his mouth, sucking on her with all the hunger in him.

Magnus cupped her pussy and she gasped, arching against his hand as he stroked across her clit. Her nipple hardened against Slade's tongue and he nipped gently, causing her to gasp. He turned his attention to her other breast, trying not to smile in delight as she turned into his touch, that golden hair of hers brushing the top of her ass.

He felt Magnus shift under him and wondered what the other man was up to. When Sylvia groaned he opened his eyes to find that Magnus had maneuvered himself under her and was lapping at her pussy, making her shudder.

He wanted to sink into them both, make them a part of him. He needed in ways he never had before. Slade didn't have a great deal of experience, so he was trusting his mates to tell him what they liked and what they didn't. So he watched, keeping most of his attention on Sylvia as Magnus pleasured her.

Her head fell back, her face became agonized, and she shuddered, her hips rocking back and forth over Magnus's mouth. Slade took hold of her other breast, running his thumb over and over her nipple, and her eyes flew wide as she choked out a cry.

"Mm." Magnus shifted out from under Sylvia as she collapsed against Slade, her breath coming in gasps. "She tastes wonderful."

"Show me." Slade leaned over and kissed Magnus, tasting both of his mates on Magnus's tongue. "You're right. She does."

Sylvia was watching them, her eyes glazed with want. Visions of being sandwiched between the two of them drifted through his mind, but that wasn't what he wanted today. No, Magnus had offered him something, and Slade would take it with glee. He'd be buried in his mate while Magnus pleasured their other mate. It would be his turn soon enough. He'd have his moment with Sylvia, but for now?

For now, he had a man to fuck.

"Drape your legs over the edge of the bed."

Magnus apparently knew what he had in mind, for he got into position without protest.

"Sylvia?"

"Hmm?" She was still riding the high of the orgasm Magnus had given her.

"Do you want to join in, or do you want to watch?" Nothing, *nothing* would ever force his mate's choices ever again. Not Odin, not Frederica. They would make sure she was free to do as she wished.

He shook his head, aware deep inside that both Magnus and Sylvia had been far freer than he ever had, and he planned to keep it that way.

"You don't want me to?" She sounded confused, and no wonder. His own distraction was to blame.

"Of course I do." He cupped her cheek. "I want the choice to be yours."

"You've made that clear." The sympathy in her gaze was almost his undoing. "And I've already decided, Slade, or I wouldn't be naked."

He smiled, certain now that she wanted this just as much as he did. "Then ride him. Show him you want him."

She nodded and swung her leg over Magnus, taking his cock deep within her pussy. When she bottomed out Slade groaned right along with Magnus. It was the most beautiful sight he'd seen, his two mates pleasuring one another, free of the shackles that had kept them apart for so long.

Slade kept an eye on them both as he made his way to where he knew Magnus kept the lube. He found it quickly, returning to them as Sylvia began rocking her hips, dragging her pussy over Magnus's cock.

Magnus had his hands on her hips, holding her steady while she rode him, making sure she was firmly on the bed. Slade nodded his approval as he placed the tube of lube on the bed next to them and removed his clothing. Once he was naked he picked the tube up again and popped it open, smiling when Magnus grunted. "Get me ready, Slade. I don't know how much longer I can hold out."

His voice was so strained Slade was surprised he hadn't come yet, not that he could complain. He slicked up his fingers and began slowly, gradually loosening Magnus's opening, carefully watching and listening for any signs of discomfort. While the tension seemed to ease, the obvious need to come backing off as Slade worked him, Magnus didn't look to be in any distress. If anything, he began to thrust upward, riding Slade's fingers as he slipped them into his mate.

Magnus loosened up far more easily than Slade liked. Had he had a lover recently, or did he use toys on himself?

If it was the latter Slade would like to see that. If it was the former, Slade…

Hell. Slade would just have to get over it. Now was not the time to think about it. Now was the time to finally claim what was his.

"Ready for me?"

"More than. Sylvia?"

She nodded. "It won't hurt, will it?"

Even in the midst of her own pleasure she thought of Magnus's comfort. Slade smiled and leaned over to kiss her shoulder. "I swear, I won't hurt him."

"All right." She shuddered as Magnus stilled. "All for one and one for all."

Slade chuckled and removed his fingers from Magnus's opening. "The three Musketeers, fighting for justice."

"And cookies." Magnus blinked when Sylvia laughed. "What?"

Slade slicked up his cock, adding more lube than he thought he needed. He'd rather be safe than make Magnus sorry he'd agreed to this. He pressed the head of his cock to Magnus's opening and blew out a nervous breath. He wanted to fuck this up in the good way, not the bad. "Okay."

"Hey." He glanced over Sylvia's shoulder to find Magnus grinning. "You lubed me, and you, you stretched me out, waited for me to be ready… Slade, you're doing fine. I'll tell you if you do something I don't like, I swear it."

"And I'll watch his face, make sure he's not hurting and trying to hide it." Sylvia lifted off Magnus's cock and slammed down hard. "Or he won't get any more of that."

Magnus's eyes crossed. "Grk."

Slade eased into Magnus, trusting the pair of them to let him know if he did anything wrong. When neither of them stopped him and he bottomed out, he breathed a sigh of relief. He hadn't hurt Magnus, and Sylvia, who'd been glancing between the pair of them, seemed more turned on than ever.

He kissed her the next time she twisted toward him, the position awkward, the kiss sloppy and somehow perfect. He kept one hand on Magnus's hip and cupped her breast in the other. "Ride him. Let's show him why he waited for us."

"I know why."

But they ignored Magnus, taking him between them, Slade inside him and Sylvia wrapped around him. Slade did his best to keep them connected, caressing Sylvia as he took Magnus, stroking her hair, her back, her breasts, anything to let her know that the three of them were in this together.

When Magnus pulled out the dagger, the one Slade had used to bind them together, he knew what Magnus was up to. He tugged on Sylvia's hand, and she allowed him to draw the blade across her palm.

What he didn't expect was for Magnus to do the same to Slade's. "You know what to do."

Slade did. Shuddering at the knowledge that Magnus was granting him the right to bond Sylvia first, he held out his bleeding hand. His hips jerked as Sylvia slowly joined their hands together. "Blood to blood, we are one."

Sylvia nodded, her eyes filled with tears. "One."

Magnus merely smiled and grabbed hold of Sylvia's hips. "Now finish it, Slade."

Slade felt the tingle of Sylvia's magic flowing through him along with her blood. It was heady, golden, filling him with savage joy. He began to pound into Magnus once more, earning a groan from his lover.

"Oh. Oh, yes." Sylvia also began to ride Magnus harder than before, taking her pleasure from his hard cock. At one point she stopped, rotating her hips, rubbing her swollen clit on the red hair that surrounded his cock, teasing them both.

Magnus allowed it. He allowed it all, watching them both with such love, such desire, that Slade had to bite the inside of his cheek to keep from blowing too soon. No. He wanted, needed, Magnus to go off before he did.

But it was Sylvia who gave in to the pleasure first, her head falling back as she shuddered above Magnus. Sharp, short cries spilled from her lips, her breasts thrust forward into Slade's hands. Her hair, that golden, glorious, magical hair, spilled down her back. For the first time ever Slade experienced that magic as it caressed him, wrapping him up in its shimmering strands. Slade succumbed to the ecstasy, pouring into Magnus with his own hoarse shout.

It seemed to be too much for Magnus. With a sharp cry he pulled Sylvia tightly to him, his orgasm causing his ass to wrap so tightly around Slade's cock Slade thought he might come again.

Sylvia collapsed over Magnus, her hair pulling away from Slade and returning to its normal appearance. "Wow."

Slade nodded, unable to speak. He was shaken by Magnus's gift. Now Slade belonged to both of them, in a bond no one could break, not even Odin.

He finally belonged, right where he'd always wanted to be.

He pulled out of Magnus, collapsing next to him, face first in the pillow. And he smiled when both of his lovers kissed him softly on the head.

The warm afterglow was shattered by the explosion of the wards blowing. The entire building shook, causing Magnus to clutch both Sylvia and Slade close. Sylvia screamed, the wave of hot and cold jotun magic washing over her, fighting each other in a wave of agonizing pain.

"Fuck." Slade was the first to react, his face pale, getting off the bed so quickly she didn't even see him move. The whites of his eyes had almost completely disappeared. "Get up and get dressed. I think Skadi is making a house call."

Sylvia shivered, her skin still burning with conflicting jotun magic. "This is not good. She'll go after Logan and Kir."

Magnus snarled as he got up. "She'll try and kill Jordan and the babies."

The two men exchanged a quick glance before tugging her from the bed. Magnus began giving orders. "Slade take Sylvia and find Kir. I'm going to find Logan and see what needs to be done."

"If Odin senses the wards are down he'll try and come through." Slade was shaking like a leaf, but he kept moving, dressing quickly. His eyes, though, remained shifted, another sign of his distress. "He won't be able to resist."

"How did Skadi get through?" Sylvia tossed on a maxi dress, forgoing underwear in favor of speed. She slid her feet into flats in case she needed to run outside. "Logan's wards were damn strong."

"I don't know." Magnus grabbed for her as an aftershock rocked the building, nearly knocking her off her feet. "She had to have help."

Slade tugged Sylvia's hand, running toward the front door. She could hear the voices of some of the others now, the shouts of dismay clear.

"It has to be another ice jotun, one strong enough to battle Logan. She'd never get one of the fire jotun to help her." Magnus yanked open the front door, putting out his hand to stop them from leaving the condo. He peered outside before stepping through the door. "Coast is clear."

Slade nodded and dashed toward Kir, Logan and Jordan's condo, Sylvia's hand held tightly in his own. "Find out what's going on."

"Sylvia!"

Sylvia tugged Slade to a stop at the sound of Sydney's panicked voice. "Syd!" She pulled free of Slade's grasp and ran toward Sydney. "Are you okay?"

"I'm fine." Syd grabbed hold of Sylvia, her eyes wide with terror. "Is it Odin?"

"I think it's Skadi." She was still shivering from the blast of ice magic. "We need to get to Jordan."

Syd's eyes went wide before a determined look took over, one Sylvia knew well. "We have to protect the babies."

Sylvia nodded. They might not be warriors, but Sylvia was both a fertility goddess and the goddess of motherhood. Sydney was the steadfast one, the goddess of fidelity, the one whose loyalty was unshakeable. It was why she'd had such a hard time giving up the dream of Logan, and why she would protect Jordan with everything in her, keeping Logan's children safe no matter what.

"Get inside, you two." Kir was suddenly there, his gaze filled with dark clouds as Baldur roused. His voice had a booming, echoing quality to it that had both Sydney and Sylvia scurrying for his front door.

"I'll protect them, I swear it." Sylvia glanced back to see Slade kiss Magnus on the cheek. "Be careful. We need you in one piece."

Magnus nodded, cupping Slade's cheek while his gaze darted toward Sylvia. "I will."

It was as much as she could ask for. Magnus was already turning toward his twin, the brothers holding out their hands, the glow of power surrounding them familiar yet different. *Mjolnir* appeared between them, the hammer of Thor spinning slightly before landing in Morgan's outstretched hand.

Sylvia opened the door to Logan's condo and shoved Sydney through. "C'mon. We have a pregnant woman to take care of."

"I can take care of myself, thanks." Jordan stood there, her arms crossed over her very pregnant belly, her glasses halfway down her nose as she glared at them. She pushed the glasses up and sighed. "But I suppose I could use some company."

Slade slipped through the door and shut it behind him. "Hey."

Jordan's smile was weak. "Hey."

Sylvia shivered as a wave of ice magic washed over her again. "Do you know what's going on?"

Jordan nodded sharply. "It is Skadi, Logan confirmed it. He's out there now, trying to reestablish the wards before Odin figures out they're down."

"Is Odin with her?" Sydney bit her lip, her gaze darting around. Syd was more terrified of Odin than she was of Vali.

"I can't sense him in the magic, if that helps." Jordan waddled toward the sofa and lowered herself carefully down. "And I'm too far along to help with the wards. Logan says it could hurt the babies if I try." For just a moment, fire danced in Jordan's eyes, letting Sylvia know that she'd gotten Logan's fire powers. "I can tell that there's more than one magic signature, so she's not alone."

"Great." Sylvia plopped down next to Jordan and extended her senses. "The babies are doing fine, by the way. They're nervous because you are, but they're otherwise comfortable."

For a second profound relief crossed Jordan's face. "Thank you. Kir tells me that all the time, but..."

"But you were afraid he'd lie to you for your piece of mind?" Sylvia took hold of Jordan's hand. "I know one of them is Kir's and the other is Logan's, but because they're sharing blood in the womb they'll each have some of the other's gifts."

Jordan smiled. "Good. I want them to be brothers in every sense of the word."

Sylvia blinked. "Brothers?"

Jordan opened her mouth to respond, but the condo got rocked again by battling magic. "Damn it!" She growled, a truly impressive sound. She must have been taking lessons from Fenris, because she sounded just as fierce as the werewolf. "Slade, check and see what's going on."

Slade nodded, obeying without a murmur. He slipped outside, shutting the door behind him.

"Sydney, get online and get word out to Nik DeWitt. Tell him Toni is under attack."

"Got it." Syd raced for Logan's computer room. If anyone could get hold of the elusive Guardian it was Syd.

"What did you mean when you said 'brothers'?" Sylvia tried to hide her smile. "What makes you think you're having boys?"

"Because only men could make me this miserable?" Jordan glared down at her stomach. "I need some pineapple juice. You want some?"

Sylvia shuddered. Jordan's obsession with pineapples had lasted the entire pregnancy. The condo smelled like happy hour at Margaritaville. "No thanks."

"Your loss." Jordan shuffled into the kitchen. "So. Boys or girls?"

"Yes." Sylvia smiled. "One of each."

"Really? We need to go over those baby names again." Jordan hobbled back, clutching a glass of yellow juice, and settled back on the sofa.

"What names did you pick?" Sylvia winced as she heard the distinct sounds of battle outside the door. Where the hell was Slade? He hadn't returned. Had he gotten caught up in the assault?

Jordan glanced toward the door, her face pale. "Anders and Rune."

"Rune could work for a girl." Sylvia tried to ignore what was going on outside the condo, instead focusing solely on Jordan. "Rune Saeter sounds lovely."

"It does, doesn't it?" Jordan rubbed her tummy, a sweet smile on her face.

Rune might be a male name in Norway, but here in America it would suit a female perfectly. "Anders is also a good one."

"I'm trying to talk them into another R-name, but Kir is in love with the name Anders, so I think I'll wind up losing that battle."

"Who picked Rune?"

"Logan did, but I loved it too." Jordan sighed. "I like both names, really. Andy and Rune." She leaned back against the sofa and closed her eyes. "Andy and Rune."

The longing and love in her voice brought tears to Sylvia's eyes. "They'll be here soon. They want to see their mama."

Jordan smiled, but didn't open her eyes. "Let's hope they get the chance."

Sylvia glanced toward the front door once again. *Where the hell is Slade?*

When the front door opened, she thought she'd finally get her answer.

Chapter Ten

Magnus raced to stand beside Logan. Damn it, they'd breached the corridor, almost making it to the condos. "The wards?"

"Working on it." Logan was tense, his hands waving, his brow dotted with sweat. "She keeps breaking it right back down."

He rocked back on his heels as Skadi slammed them with another wave of magic. Logan's magic flared around them, fire against ice, the two evenly matched. "How the hell did she convince the other jotuns to give her aid?"

Logan gritted his teeth as Magnus tossed *Mjolnir* to Morgan. "She must have promised them something big to get them to go against me."

"Kir's heading back to your condo to watch over the girls." Magnus nodded to Fenris and Jeff, both in their wolf forms. Jeff glowed with the bright light of the *Lios Alfar*, a gift he'd received from sharing blood with his sister, Jamie. She, too, was in the battle, surprising them all with the bolts of pure light that flew from her hands.

"Good." Logan looked relieved. "I want Blondie out of this." He gasped as a particularly strong thrust of ice magic wrapped around him.

Magnus gestured toward Morgan, who tossed *Mjolnir* back to him. Using his powers, Magnus focused his lightning through the hammer, shattering the ice that surrounded Logan.

"Thanks." Logan grinned and focused once more on the battle, something Magnus should have been doing.

Ice jotuns were coming out of the damned woodwork, fighting the Aesir everywhere he looked. Even Skye had joined in the fray, twirling a staff in front of her and shielding the door to Jordan's home. Travis glowed brighter than the sun as he battled…

"Is that *Hrym?* Isn't he supposed to be on our side?" Magnus tossed *Mjolnir* to Morgan, who cracked a frost jotun over the head.

"Who the fuck knows! None of this has made sense since it started." Morgan swung the hammer, blocking a blow from a jotun.

Magnus darted across the hall, the narrow environs making the battle more difficult. This was no open field, but the doors to their homes, the enemy trying to get as close to Logan as they could. Arrows flew as those jotun in the rear took aim, only to be thwarted by Jamie's magic. She shielded Logan, the icy arrows bouncing off and landing feet away, only to melt into the carpet within seconds.

Magnus threw lightning at a jotun threatening Jamie, gaining his attention. His opponent rushed Magnus, but Magnus responded with more lightning, laughing when *Mjolnir* slammed into the back of the jotun's head. "Thanks." *Mjolnir* landed in his hand.

"Welcome." Morgan ducked a blow from a jotun spear. "A little help here, please."

Magnus tossed *Mjolnir*, killing the jotun who'd taken aim at his brother. But despite their best efforts, the Aesir were slowly being forced back.

Jeff's condo was the first to be breached, the frost jotuns immediately darting in and tearing the place apart. Jeff howled in rage and ran after them, followed closely by his mate. Blood sprayed from the doorway, and Magnus could only hope it was the enemy's blood and not his brother's.

One by one doors were opened as the Aesir were forced to give ground. Magnus had no doubt their adversaries were seeking Jordan and the children she carried. If they could destroy her and the lives she held, Kir and Logan would break.

It was a sound strategy, but one that would fail if Magnus had anything to say about it.

When Logan fell under a barrage not even Jamie could halt, he thought maybe he wouldn't get the chance to say anything at all. They were losing, and now Skadi, free of the battle against Logan, was wading into the fight. The female held her head high, her eyes blazing with triumph as she made her way to her fallen enemy, ready to end him once and for all.

Magnus and Morgan did their best to batter aside as many of the jotun as they could, desperately hoping they would make it to Logan's side before it was too late, but Magnus already knew they wouldn't make it. Skadi lifted her sword high, and started to bring it down.

A loud *bang* filled the air, and Skadi staggered back, her sword almost falling from her hand.

"Freeze! On the ground, *now*!"

Magnus knew exactly who had just decided to join the battle, and he was terrified. If anything happened to Toni, Nik would kick their asses all the way to Niflheim. He continued to try and battle his way toward Skadi, hoping to head off a battle between the jotun and the human.

Skadi laughed and raised her sword again. "Interesting choice of words, mortal, but I think not."

The human surprised him. Toni dashed past him so quickly he barely saw her. Her guns blazing, she took down more jotun than any of the rest of them combined.

"Shit. Her valkyrie blood is kicking in." Morgan paled. "We have to stop her."

"No shit." Magnus threw *Mjolnir*, hoping to hit Skadi, but it boomeranged back to him when Skadi ducked.

But that missed swing left her open for Toni's blow. The guns in her hands blazed with the fiery light of the valkyries, Toni's chosen weapons becoming extensions of her arms. They roared like mini dragons, spitting fire and lead at the ice jotun.

Skadi, her expression startled, tried her best to dodge the incoming hail of bullets, but more struck her than not. Bleeding from numerous wounds inflicted within seconds, she dropped her sword and lurched back, damn near tripping over one of her fellow jotuns.

"Go Toni!" Jamie was jumping up and down, pumping her arms like a maniac.

Toni raced around, firing at Hrym before turning her guns once more on Skadi. Her movements were a blur, the spurt of blood from her victims the only sign that she'd hit what she'd aimed at.

And she did, almost all of the time. None of the jotun could move as quickly as she could, and Toni's entrance into the battle turned the tide in the favor of the Aesir. Magnus and Morgan followed behind her, mopping up the few jotun who managed to stay on their feet. While Toni aimed to disable, Magnus and Morgan killed, the thrill of battle singing in their blood.

"Retreat!" Hrym sounded the call, ignoring Skadi's snarl of protest. "Now, woman! We are done here."

Magnus's heart froze in his chest.

"Jordan?"

Before he could panic, Slade was next to him, spattered in blood. Why his mate was out here instead of protecting Jordan, Sylvia and Sydney, he didn't know. "They're safe. Kir's with them." Slade was breathing hard and clutching his side. Magnus realized not all of the blood on his mate belonged to their enemies.

He watched as the jotun fled, leaving Logan behind. Travis and Jamie stood over the fallen man, guarding him in a shield of light, thwarting Skadi's last attempt to end Logan's life.

"Well. That was fun. What's next, bowling for psychos?" Toni holstered her guns, and only then did Magnus see she'd strapped on holsters remarkably similar to those worn by Lara Croft. "What the fuck just happened here?"

Fenris stepped out of his condo, Jeff leaning against him heavily, his arm cradled to him. "That was another little taste of Ragnarrok, I think."

Toni grunted and stared around at the bodies with a mixture of disgust and dismay. "Great. How the hell am I going to explain this to the chief?"

"You won't." Travis carefully lifted Logan in his arms, the fire jotun still unconscious. "We will. If there's anything left to explain, that is."

"What are you talking about?" Toni was walking the battlefield, still glowing slightly. As her light touched each body, it would shiver. Magnus watched as the jotun dead disappeared one by one, to go to their final rewards in either Valhalla or Hel.

Considering they'd all attacked on Odin's orders, he was willing to bet their souls were headed for Odin's palace, there to await the final battle.

"Whoa." Toni stopped dead in her tracks, watching the last body fade and disappear. "Did… Did I do that?"

Jeff let go of Fenris and put his arm around her shoulder. "I would like to officially welcome you to Dysfunction Junction."

Fenris took his place on Jeff's other side. "As I said. You are family, Antonia."

"Toni." She grimaced. "It's going to get worse, isn't it?"

Travis nodded. "It will."

Magnus saw the grief on her face. "We'll be there for you, Toni."

Morgan winked. "You belong with us now."

Jamie hugged her. "We can bake cookies together!"

Toni huffed out a laugh. "Right. Cookies." She allowed herself to be dragged toward Logan and Kir's condo. "Remind me why I put up with this?"

"Because we're cute?" Jeff blinked up at her innocently.

Even as she shook her head, Toni touched Jeff's arm, healing the wound.

Yup. As much as Toni wanted to deny it, she was now theirs.

***

"Damn it, it's not working." Logan ran his fingers through his thick hair, his frustration causing flames to lick up and down his arms.

"We'll figure this out." Sydney reached out and put her hand on his arm, causing Kir to snarl before he turned away.

"Couldn't do it without you." Logan patted her hand, but his gaze was glued to Kir, who didn't seem to notice.

Logan was still attempting to put the wards back up a week later. The makeshift wards Jordan had cobbled together with Tyr weren't enough for the fire jotun. Skadi and her crew of ice jotuns had gotten far too close to his pregnant wife for his comfort, and he was working night and day to figure out ways to keep that from happening again. Sydney had offered her assistance, surprising all of them except Sylvia. She'd known Sydney would want to do whatever she could to help. What was giving the two so much grief was the fact none of them had ice magic in their veins, so Logan couldn't test the new wards against it.

Sydney was working on a solution that could mimic ice magic, but they wouldn't be absolutely sure it worked until they were attacked again. Logan was going to worry himself into an early grave at this rate, immortal god or not.

Jordan was in the kitchen, grumbling and slamming pots down. Kir went after her, but Logan only sighed and began speaking quietly to Sydney again.

Sylvia waited until Morgan and Slade were distracted and slipped into the kitchen, determined to make things right with Kir, Logan and Jordan. "Hey."

The two, who'd cuddled close, grimaced. "Hi," Kir responded.

Jordan put her head on his shoulder with a weary sigh. "Hi."

Sylvia grinned and blocked the door out of the kitchen. She didn't want one of them bolting from her before she got to the bottom of what was going on between them. "You guys all right?"

Jordan shook her head no even as Kir nodded yes. "I want to pluck her blonde hair out."

Sylvia chuckled. "She's got a crush on Val."

Kir blinked. "What? She hides behind whatever warm body is in the room whenever Val is here. I mean, look at her." He pointed toward the living room, and Sylvia stifled a laugh. Syd kept maneuvering herself so that Logan was always between her and the glowering Val.

Jordan was smiling, though. "I thought she might like him, but then she started hanging on Logan and…"

"And little green monsters started dancing all around?" Sylvia nodded sympathetically. "I could see why you'd be worried. She's his ex, and they're spending all this time together. But I can tell you that she's more worried about you than about Logan." The snort of disgust was amusing, but Jordan had nothing to be worried about. "Logan adores the ground you walk on. And we already know he'd give his life for both of you. Syd wants to prevent that, just like you do."

Kir nodded. Despite his words he looked relieved. "And she's upset that Jordan was in danger."

"Exactly." Sylvia was watching them both closely, saw how Jordan leaned into Kir. "She worries for those babies, you know."

"Why? I don't get it." Jordan began to frown again, but this time it wasn't in anger.

Sylvia closed her eyes, remembering the horror that had been inflicted not only on Logan but on Syd. "The children who were mutilated to tie Loki to the mountain were hers as well as his."

Jordan paled as Kir quietly confirmed Sylvia's words. "He doesn't like to talk about it. It hurts too much."

"And Syd, well…" Sylvia shrugged. "She's been trying to break free of the Old Man and Frederica ever since, but their hold was too strong. It wasn't until Kir got hold of the god spear that we were truly freed of his influence." Sylvia stepped forward and put her hand on Jordan's shoulder. "We're both sorrier than we can say."

It was Kir who hugged her, and until he wiped away a tear she hadn't even realized she'd begun crying. "We've forgiven all of you."

"Has she grieved?" Jordan glanced toward the doorway, her expression full of sadness.

"Every day of her life." Sylvia had heard Sydney crying at night, calling for her dead children, but they never spoke of it. Syd did everything she could to live her life, but nothing could totally erase her grief. "But Syd is strong, stronger than she gives herself credit for. Everything she does, she does so this will *never* happen to someone else's child. Odin will never have that power again."

"Does seeing Logan ease some of that?"

She almost laughed at the expression on Jordan's face. The poor woman looked ready to staple Syd to Logan's side. "A little, yes, but I think it has more to do with seeing Logan with you and Kir. I think, for her, it's one less thing she has to worry about. Logan is taken care of, so she can make sure that the people who make him happy are taken care of."

"So she still loves him." Kir was obviously confused.

"Not the way you two do, but yes, she does. Of course she does. She's the goddess of fidelity, remember? She'll always have a special place for Logan in her heart." Sylvia hugged the two of them tight and whispered in their ears. "But it's Val who makes her crazy now, not Logan. Look at the way they're working together and you'll see it. It's like two old friends trying to solve a puzzle, not two old lovers trying to score with each other."

"And the only one she has trouble talking to is Val." Jordan snickered. "And he has no idea why." In fact, from the death glares he was shooting Logan's way, perhaps he should be in here talking to them instead of trying to commit murder with his eyeballs.

"So he keeps trying to talk to her, hoping she'll like him?" Kir bit his lip, a look of unholy amusement on his face. "Should we pass notes for them?"

"We can put their initials in hearts on their Trapper Keepers." Jordan shared a look with Kir, and they burst into laughter.

"What's going on in here?"

Sylvia shook her head at the pair before turning to answer Logan. He was staring at his lovers, partly relieved, partly worried. "They're idiots."

He huffed out a laugh. "I knew that, but what has them in stitches?"

"It's a secret."

He eyed them for a moment. "Mm-hm." He shook his head. "Syd has an idea on how to test the wards. We're going to run a simulation. She thinks it will work, but I'm not as sure." He approached them, and Sylvia backed up, giving her spot to Logan. "I want you two to settle on the sofa and hold on, just in case."

As the three began talking quietly to one another, Sylvia left them to it. The moment she entered the living room Magnus and Slade were there, studying her with equal degrees of concern and amusement. Magnus, as usual, spoke before Slade. "Is everything all right?"

"Are *they* all right?" Slade's tone was gruffer than usual, the rasp more prominent.

"They're fine." She caressed his cheek, smiling as he leaned into her touch. She did the same for Magnus, the smile becoming wider as he kissed her palm. "They're working something out, that's all."

"Syd and Logan?" Magnus's sharp gaze hadn't missed the interactions between Logan and Syd, or Kir and Jordan's reaction to it.

"They have nothing to worry about, and now they know for sure why." Sylvia took her men by the hand and led them to the huge white sofa.

"Care to tell the rest of the class?" Slade settled her down before taking the seat next to her. Magnus perched on the ottoman across from them, his gaze focusing on the pair of them with an odd satisfaction.

He liked this, liked being able to see Sylvia and Slade together, the protector in him soothed by the knowledge that they were safe. She could see that in him, that glimpse of the warrior mingling with the man who desperately wanted a family, how it manifested in this way. He was very pleased they were there, where he could guard them, and he did nothing to hide that from them.

Slade, on the other hand, nudged her knee. "Well?"

"It's a secret." She smiled serenely when he glared at her.

He leaned forward and kissed her nose. "Syd and Val?"

She blinked, shocked. "How did you know?"

He winked and leaned back. "When you've done nothing but watch for as long as I have, you either become very observant, or you blind yourself to everything around you."

"Blinding yourself would have made you vulnerable."

"Exactly." Slade put his hand on her knee, the need to touch as obvious as Magnus's need to protect. He coughed, a quick frown of pain crossing his face, before he spoke again. "I think Val would be willing if she'd allow it."

"What makes you say that?"

"He watches her." Slade said no more, either because his throat was hurting him again or because that was all he felt needed to be said.

Magnus stood, eyeing Slade with concern. "I'll get you some tea. Lemon or honey?"

"Honey."

Sylvia put her arms around Slade. He only asked for honey when his throat *really* hurt. He sighed, resting his head on top of hers, cuddling with her on the sofa. "It's okay. Everything will work out." He snickered. "Including Val and Syd."

"Can I bring the popcorn?" She giggled against his chest.

"Only if I can bring the Goobers."

Sylvia giggled harder as she saw Syd begin dancing away from Val once more, to the Avenger's obvious frustration. "Hate to tell you this, but they're already here."

Chapter Eleven

They practically danced into the condo later that day. Sylvia giggled as Slade kissed her, her entire being flooding with light. It was like drinking espresso made from Red Bull and rainbows, and sweetened with fresh honey. It was the warm taste of Slade, the wind in her hair as she ran, the freedom and joy of racing against the wind itself. It was the magic of the shape-shifting jotun, and the knowledge that she too could ride the wind was heady to her. One day, she'd be able to test what she already knew, would fly beside her white-haired mate and rejoice in the sky together.

And then there was Magnus, always Magnus, his fierce desire burning into her. Even though they had yet to bond, she could almost grasp the essence of him in her hands. The man was pure lighting. Fierce and hot and dazzling, a lightshow to some, a fierce force of nature to others, Magnus was all of that, and more.

Sylvia could feel someone's hands on her waist and instantly knew who had hold of her. "Lay down, sweetheart," Magnus's dark voice whispered in her ear. The man was pure sex, from the way his green eyes blazed into hers to his hands sliding up her sides to cup her breasts. "Let us love on you."

Oh, she was so totally down for that one. Sylvia quickly complied, lying on her back and letting go of Slade's hand. Slade leaned over, taking her mouth in a kiss designed to set her soul on fire. He lifted his mouth from hers and looked over at their other mate. "Taste her, Magnus."

Magnus's brows rose, but he carefully moved Slade off him before sliding down the bed. Sylvia eagerly shifted, parting her thighs for him. She couldn't wait to feel his tongue doing wicked things…to…

Oh.

Oh.

Slade was nibbling his way down the side of her neck, pausing at the junction between her neck and shoulder to suck up a mark. She shuddered under him.

"Magnus? I think I found a hot spot on our pretty mate."

Magnus chuckled. "Mark it well so I can find it when it's my turn."

"Already done, my mate."

The feel of Magnus's tongue on her clit was better than she'd ever imagined. Never had she had a lover as attentive as he to her desires. He held her hips down and took her clit into his mouth, sucking it in, sipping at the folds, drawing her essence inside him.

When Slade began playing with her breasts, nipping at her tender skin and drawing her hard nipples into his hot mouth she had a hard time not coming right then and there. "Let me suck you."

Slade whimpered. "No. Not yet."

She blinked, startled. She'd never had a man turn down a blowjob before. She glanced at her lover, startled to see that the whites of his eyes were almost completely obscured. He was shuddering as he stroked her nipples, his body rocking back and forth.

She suddenly realized why Slade was so close to coming himself. Sneaky Magnus had apparently gotten the lube and was preparing Slade while eating her pussy. He was fucking himself on Magnus's fingers while pleasuring her.

It was an erotic sight, watching Slade's enjoyment as he gave her the same. Not once while Magnus took care of them both did Slade forget her, touching and teasing with strokes both gentle and hard. He kept kissing her, her mouth, her flesh, tasting every inch of her he could reach, driving her insane with need.

"In her, sweetness." Magnus stopped just as Sylvia was ready to beg him to let her come. "Fuck our mate for me."

Slade nodded eagerly. "Yes, fuck yes." The two men switched places, Magnus kissing her, their taste mingled on his tongue.

Slade's cock slid inside her, filling her, stretching her in all the right ways. She brushed his hair back from his face and smiled. "Hey."

He kissed the tip of her nose as he bottomed out. "Hey." His eyes went wide and he shivered. "Oh." He hung his head, panting slightly, his cock throbbing inside her.

Magnus was behind him, leaning over them both and carefully taking the man beneath him. "You're so tight, Slade."

Slade hissed, his expression blissful. "Fuck."

"Most definitely." Magnus grinned at Sylvia over Slade's shoulder, his hands landing next to Slade's beside her head. "C'mon, sweetness. Let's rock his world."

"With our socks on?" She chuckled, causing both men to moan as they shifted.

Slade was the first to move, as if he couldn't stop himself, sliding in and out of her in quick, short motions that didn't satisfy but teased. Magnus took that as the signal that he, too, could start moving, fucking Slade with an intensity that had Slade gasping in pleasure.

Slade stared down at Sylvia, his expression predatory. "Wrap your legs around us."

She blinked and tried to comply, but the two men together were just too thick. So instead, she widened her legs, her feet planted on the mattress as she met Slade thrust for thrust. She felt it begin, that slow build up that heralded her orgasm, her whole body clenching and unclenching around Slade's cock.

"Yes, that's it," Slade hissed. "Come for me." He reached between them and thumbed her clit, sending her over the edge into oblivion. She came screaming, her toes curling, her nails digging into Slade's shoulders as she rocked against him, dragging the pleasure on and on until she thought she'd pass out.

"Oh, shit," Slade gasped. His mouth opened in a silent scream of his own, his hands clenching and unclenching beside her head as he filled her with his come.

"Oh, fuck, yeah, come, Slade. Come for me, baby." Magnus was gasping for breath, his eyes wide. "Come on, come on." He cried out, shuddering over them, his eyes clenched shut. He grunted, stilling as he, too, was overcome with ecstasy.

Sylvia relaxed, totally sated, as her lovers carefully pulled out. Slade fell over, his hair damp, his eyes closed and a serene smile on his full red lips.

Magnus, on the other hand, carefully squirmed in between them, laying on his stomach so that he could hug both of them to him. "Let's go again."

Slade grunted, but didn't speak, his eyes still closed.

Sylvia, on the other hand, lifted her fist into the air wearily. "Rock on."

Both men laughed, but none of them moved for at least twenty minutes. But when they did, when they slipped and slid against one another, arms and legs tangling in a dance older than time itself, rocks were gotten off rather than on.

Sylvia could more than live with that.

***

Magnus woke to an interesting, yet familiar, sensation. "Ow."

"Shh. Don't wake Sylvia." Slade's reply was barely audible.

"What are you doing?" Magnus opened one eye to see Slade standing over him with a knife. He blinked and held still, praying his balls would reappear sometime in the future. They'd decided to curl up and hide from the possibilities to be found in the things Slade held. "I'm sorry?"

Slade blinked, looking confused, before he rolled his eyes. "You have to claim Sylvia."

Well. His morning was looking slightly brighter. He relaxed, his anus unclenching and his balls peeking out to make sure the coast was clear. "Ah." He should have realized sooner. As a shifter, Slade would feel the need to mark both his mates, but, unlike Fenris, he didn't have fangs. Perhaps, once Magnus finally claimed Sylvia and cemented their three-way bond, Slade would let go of his fear of losing them.

It would take more than the blood bond to get rid of the rest of Slade's nightmares, but with time and enough love Magnus hoped they'd at least lessen in intensity. He doubted they'd ever go away completely.

"What did you think I was doing?" Slade was gloriously naked, the soft tuft of fur around his cock damp. He'd obviously cleaned himself in preparation for this.

"Nothing." He swallowed as Slade got onto the bed, swinging his leg over Magnus until he was sitting on his hips. Magnus's cock was tucked tightly against Slade's ass, twitching at the feel of the firm globes gliding over him. "Not a damn thing."

"Please tell me you're not reenacting that Sharon Stone ice pick scene." Sylvia's sleepy voice had him turning his head, only to find her with her eyes closed and a soft smile on her lips. "That's just wrong."

Slade was staring at her like she was crazy, so Magnus explained gently while holding on to Slade's hips. If he knew his lover the man would try to climb off of him, and Magnus was enjoying his wiggling far too much to allow that. "The knife, baby." Sure enough Slade tried to climb off of him. "Just put it on the end table."

Sylvia rolled onto her back and stretched, the tank top she'd worn to bed riding up and showing a thin strip of glorious skin. "What's up, guys?" She giggled as she looked at Slade's erection. "Other than that, I mean."

Slade smiled and put the knife on the bedside table. "I want Magnus to blood bond with you, if you'll allow it."

Sylvia tilted her head. "Can we do it together?" She frowned thoughtfully. "I know Magnus and I still need to bond, but it feels...right, if we're all connected. Six palms together, Magnus to me, you to Magnus, me to you both."

Magnus had to think that one through. "We'd need to be positioned so that we could reach our hands together all at once."

Slade shrugged. "It could be fun, right?"

"Like bedroom gymnastics." Sylvia and Slade were staring at each other, but Magnus didn't care. Slade was rocking his hips back and forth, dragging Magnus's cock along his crack.

They could talk about anything they wanted as long as Slade never stopped.

Slade rubbed his hand down Magnus's chest, tweaking his nipple. "We could break out the Barbie and G.I. Joes and see how it would work best."

Sylvia curled on to her side and began stroking Magnus's arm, almost purring as she traced his biceps. "We'll need Roadblock for Magnus."

Magnus tossed Slade off like yesterday's underwear and took hold of Sylvia's arms. "You like G.I. Joe?"

"Asshole!" Slade's head peeked over the edge of the bed, but Magnus ignored him. Besides, Slade was adorable when he was mad.

"Duh. The Rock was in it." Sylvia shivered hard, practically drooling all over her pillow.

Magnus whimpered. "I love you." A sharp slap against his ass had him glaring over his shoulder. "Do you mind? I'm kind of having a moment here."

Slade glared at him as he got back on the bed. "I can't believe you did that."

Magnus stared at Slade. "The. *Rock.*"

"Yeah, what's wrong with you?"

Slade crossed his arms over his chest, his bottom lip pooching out. "You want a big guy and not me?"

"Aw, baby." Magnus grabbed hold of Slade and pulled him down. "You know you're perfect."

"But the *Rock.*" Sylvia giggled when Slade glared at her. "I like Captain America too, you know."

Magnus slid his arms around Slade, who was trying to get off the bed. "She's right. You are built like Captain America."

Sylvia nodded. "He's no slouch in the muscle department."

"Ooh, and those eyes." Magnus fanned himself.

"My eyes are black, you heifers." Slade slumped against Magnus. "You suck."

"Only if you ask nicely." Magnus batted his lashes at Slade, grinning when a slow smile came over the other man's face. "Aw, c'mon, baby. You know you're adorable."

"Hmph."

Sylvia reached over and pushed back Slade's hair. "I love this."

"My hair?"

"No." Sylvia's expression turned pensive. "That when we're all together, we feel comfortable laughing and playing with each other. I've never had that before."

"I've never had anything," Slade whispered, laying his head on Magnus's chest.

"We're hoping to make this a regular thing, for all of us." Magnus took hold of Sylvia's hand, making sure he had contact with both of them.

"Promise me something." Slade didn't look at either of them. "Promise me we'll keep laughing together."

"We can't, but I can promise that we'll do our best." Sylvia gave Slade a soft kiss.

"Ditto." Magnus also kissed Slade, his mate's taste filling his senses.

Slade nodded and sat up, once again straddling Magnus's hips. He picked up the knife and slashed Magnus's palm. "Then don't make me wait any longer. Claim each other. Please."

Sylvia didn't bat an eyelash. She took hold of the knife and did the same thing to her own palm, the shallow cuts causing her to wince. "Ditto."

"Let's rock on with our socks on."

"I don't think that's how that quote goes." But Sylvia placed her hand in his, allowing him to hold her steady.

"Does it matter?" Slade looked like a kid at Christmas as he took hold of both Sylvia and Magnus's hands. "You're both mine."

"Blood to blood, we are one." Sylvia's eyes glowed with satisfaction as her blood mingled with Magnus's.

"Love you both, so much." Magnus wasn't certain if they heard him or not, but it didn't matter. He'd said it, and there was no going back.

They'd just have to friggin' deal with it.

Before he could do much more, Sylvia's magic swept over him. It was like being bathed in golden sunshine on a perfect spring afternoon. It was gentle, sweet and strong, like the best wine.

"Oh." Sylvia shuddered, his magic racing through her as their blood joined. Lightning flashed in her eyes, lifted her hair up in a brilliant display of power.

Slade kissed her shoulder, apparently not afraid of the tiny sparks dancing along her skin. He lifted her tank top off, revealing her breasts to Magnus's dazzled eyes. "I wonder which of your powers she got?"

Magnus laughed. "Gee, I wonder."

She laughed. "It tickles."

"Tickles?" A little spark ran up her neck, and she laughed harder, squirming a bit.

He liked it when she squirmed. Parts of her anatomy, two of his favorites if he was being totally honest, bounced when she wiggled around.

He shared a glance with Slade, who seemed to be on the same page, because the two of them reached for her sleep shorts at the same time. "I think we should have some fun."

Slade nodded. "See if we can find all of the sparks."

Magnus kissed her belly button. "Found one."

Slade, laughing wickedly, licked her right nipple. "So did I."

Sylvia lay down on her back, her hair finally coming down from its lightning high. She lifted her butt in the air just far enough that they could get her shorts off the rest of the way. "Betcha can't find them all."

"I love a challenge," Magnus sighed.

"And it's my favorite kind. Hide-and-go-seek." Slade kissed Sylvia's hip. "Three."

"Four." Magnus stroked one of the little sparks, sending it dancing along her thigh. Her gasp of pleasure was better than music to his ears. She might have gotten some mastery over electricity from him, but he was still the God of Lightning. The sparks danced to his command, flaring along her skin, his blood bond keeping his lovers safe from any harm.

"He's cheating," he heard Slade whisper to Sylvia.

"And?" She stared at him incredulously.

Slade shrugged. "Just thought I should mention it." He then nipped at her earlobe. "Five."

Magnus stroked between her thighs, delighted at the wetness he found. "Six."

Sylvia gasped as the spark stroked over her clit. No pain, only pleasure, his blood and magic making the spark a caress rather than a jolt. He fingered her, playing that little spark all over her pussy, forgetting all about the game in the need to see his lover come under his touch.

He glanced up to find Slade and Sylvia kissing, silver and gold, pale and beautiful. He smiled, the love he felt for them overwhelming him. Slade was holding her so gently, like she was the most precious person in his world.

Magnus understood how he felt. Apart, they'd almost been broken by outside forces, but together, they were far more than they could have ever been. But what Slade didn't seem to realize was that it all started with him.

Magnus lay down and placed his head on Sylvia's stomach. Still stroking her with his hand, he moved until he could pull Slade's cock into his mouth without hurting Sylvia.

Slade jumped, then groaned as Magnus worked his cock. He couldn't quite see Sylvia leaning up on her arms for a better look, but the tightening of her stomach and the way she gasped told him what she'd done.

When she reached over and helped Magnus, it was even better. She stroked what he couldn't reach, the pair of them pleasuring Slade until he was shuddering and pulling away from them.

"No. Not this time." That hoarse, sexy-as-hell voice had gone deep. He moved until his back was against the headboard, his dark eyes closed. When he opened them again, the whites were gone. "This time, it's about you two."

Magnus shared a look with Sylvia. "No."

"It's about all of us." She smiled, climbing Slade like a tree until her pussy was lined up with his cock. "All three of us. Got that?" She slid down, taking Slade into her.

"I was trying to—"

"Shh." Magnus covered Slade's mouth with his own, kissing the breath out of the man. "We know what you were doing."

He grabbed hold of her hips. "This doesn't feel like three."

"It will." Magnus whistled happily as he reached into the drawer where they kept the lube. "Just give me a moment."

Slade's eyes lit up as Magnus began to slick his cock, stroking it slowly. He was enjoying the way Sylvia and Slade were watching, like he held a delectable treat in his hands that they both wanted to devour.

"Well? What's keeping you?" Sylvia leaned over Slade and slapped her rear.

Magnus laughed as Slade's jaw dropped. "Sorry, Sylvia. We won't be doing that until we get a chance to really stretch you out."

"And by that, he means 'are you freakin' nuts?'" Slade sat up, Sylvia groaning in response as she was jostled. "He's huge."

"So are you." It was hilarious, one lover on top of the other. Sylvia's hands were now on her hips as she glared at Slade. "Hell, you're hung like a—"

"Don't say it." Slade shot her an incredulous look before darting a quick, sympathetic glance at Magnus.

He might have actually been offended if Sylvia hadn't been giggling like a loon again. "Yeah, don't make the lightning god feel inadequate." Magnus shook his head. "You two. What am I going to do with you?"

They put their heads together and gave him identical innocent looks. "Love us?"

"Hmm. Let me think about it." He dove for them, latching on to the side of Slade's neck and blowing a raspberry before doing the same to Sylvia. "Now make with the fucking, people." He reached down and wagged his slicked-up erection at them. "I'm dying of blue balls here."

"Poor baby," Sylvia cooed. She grabbed Slade and turned, pulling them until they were lying on their sides. Sliding her leg over Slade's, she repositioned herself so that she was once again impaled on his cock.

"Oh, I like where this is going." Slade slowly fucked Sylvia, his ass checks clenching and unclenching as Magnus watched.

Magnus had to palm those strong globes, feel the flex of the muscles dancing underneath the skin. The idea of the three of them connected that way was too enticing. He grabbed the bottle of lube and put a generous amount on his fingers. As Slade continued fucking Sylvia, he prepared Slade for his entry.

When he felt Slade was loose enough, he pressed the head of his cock to Slade's opening. "Ready for me?"

"Hell yes."

That gravelly tone was one Magnus was familiar with. Slade was close, ready to blow at any moment. "Sylvia?"

She shuddered, her eyes wide, her hair dancing around her head as the orgasm ripped through her.

Magnus thrust into Slade, enjoying the way Slade pushed back against him as he continued to fuck Sylvia. Sylvia's hair had bound the three of them together as they rode each other. Magnus stroked both of his lovers, touching whatever skin he could reach. Stroking the soft, golden skin of Sylvia, the lightly furred chest of Slade, he could do this forever.

It wasn't long before the primal need to come filled him, pushing him past his limits. He was the second one to come, his vision going black as the pleasure overloaded his senses. Slade's raspy cry followed as Sylvia's golden hair stroked them both.

***

Slade bit his lip as Magnus met his gaze. They were cuddling in bed, the aftermath of their lovemaking still on their skin. "I'm thinking we need to paint the bedroom ceiling."

Sylvia looked absolutely lost and completely adorable. "Huh?"

Magnus smiled sweetly. "Never mind that."

"Pfft. How can I? I'm constantly looking at it." It was *bo-ring.* Hell, his stall in Asgard had been better looking than that white nothingness.

Magnus reached over and tweaked his nipple, making Slade gasp in protest. They were sensitive after all the love play, almost painful to the touch. "I had a question for the two of you." If not for that smile Slade might have been worried. Magnus's tone was far more serious than his expression. "Where do you want to live?"

"I don't understand." Sylvia frowned, glancing between the two of them as if Slade understood exactly what Magnus was talking about.

"When this is all over and Odin is dead, where do we want to be?" Magnus glanced around. "I love it here, but let's face it. We're a little too close to one another."

"Just because a few people feel it's perfectly acceptable to walk in on us whenever they feel like it?" Slade batted his lashes at Magnus.

Magnus growled.

Slade laughed, knowing full well Magnus adored having his family nearby. "Wherever we choose we should remain close to them. I'm not quite ready to move far away from my father and brother." Slade tried to hide the shiver that came over him. Just the thought of being out there, alone except for his mates…

Nope. So not ready for that. Magnus would die to protect them, he knew that, but it wasn't something Slade ever wanted to contemplate.

"Shh." Sylvia wrapped her arms around him and began petting him, stroking his hair, his shoulders, even his hands. He didn't realize how badly he was shaking until she clasped his hand between hers to still them.

He took a deep breath and closed his eyes, trying to still his racing pulse. "I'm sorry, I just can't. Not yet."

"It's okay." The feel of Magnus's lips against his own made him open his eyes. The soft kiss was reassuring rather than heated. "We'll stay as long as you need, Slade."

"I like it here." Sylvia shrugged. "It feels like a family to me, the way it should have all along."

"Annoying?" Magnus was scowling, but Slade could tell his heart wasn't in it.

"Nosy." Slade kissed Magnus on the cheek, happy that his lover's scowl lightened at his touch.

"Crazy." Magnus twirled his finger near his temple, the universal sign for nut ball making Slade chuckle.

"Pineapple scented?"

Magnus gagged. "Please don't mention that fruit ever again."

"How about loving?" Sylvia crossed her arms over her chest and glared at them both. "Kind?"

"Psycho?" Slade ducked as Sylvia slapped him lightly on the arm, but she cuddled right back up to him after. "You know I love them all, but they're flakier than raisin bran."

Sylvia giggled.

Magnus shook his head, but placed his arm around both Slade and Sylvia, tugging them closer to him. It nearly put Sylvia in Slade's lap, but he wasn't about to complain. "So we stay here for as long as we can."

"There's room for all of us, but we might reconsider once we start having children." Sylvia blushed bright red as Slade froze.

"Kids?" His voice broke as he put his hand on her stomach. "Are you...?"

"Not yet, but if we keep at it like bunnies I will be." Sylvia didn't seem at all upset by the idea. "I'll admit, I'd like to wait until Odin is dead, but if it happens I'm—"

"Confined to the condo." Magnus was so pale he rivaled the color of Slade's hair.

"And you'll bring me whatever I want?" Sylvia leaned over Slade, her breasts pressing against Slade's side, and stroked Magnus's white cheek.

Magnus nodded, his eyes wide.

"Even pineapple?"

Magnus started to nod again, then whimpered. "Yes."

"Then I can live with being confined here." She gave him a smug smile and sat back. "Besides, I know it's because you'd be afraid for me. I'm not going to send you out to fight if you're terrified for me."

Now it was Slade's turn to whimper, but he shook his head when Magnus tried to comfort him. "I'll get over it."

"You're allowed to worry about me, Slade." Magnus glanced over at Sylvia. "About both of us. Just try not to let it to tie you up in knots."

Sylvia rubbed her cheek on his shoulder. "I'll be right here with you, worrying about Magnus too."

"We'll make sure you're not alone, Slade. Someone will always be with you." Magnus peppered his forehead with small, soothing kisses. "We're staying in the condo, forever if need be."

"And when the time comes, and we can return to Asgard, we'll be together there too."

"That's all I want." Slade's voice broke again and he swallowed, hoping it would help. "My mates, and peace."

"You'll have it, I swear." Magnus tugged and maneuvered until Slade was lying against him with Sylvia draped over them both. The warmth of his two mates surrounded him. "Even if I have to bathe the Bifrost Bridge in blood, you'll have peace."

Slade lifted himself just far enough that he could stare at Magnus. "Yup. Blood rivers are so peaceful."

"You know what I meant." Magnus poked him in his side as Sylvia giggled. "Ass."

"Your ass." And Slade couldn't be happier about that.

"Does it bother you that we aren't warriors?" Sylvia bit her lip, staring at Magnus in concern.

"Not one little bit." Magnus kissed her forehead. "You two will be the peace I need to keep my temper in check, and I'll protect you with every breath I take."

"We each have something the others need," Slade added. "Magnus makes us feel safe."

"I can make a home," Sylvia said thoughtfully.

"And Slade can teach us all about pony play." Magnus shot him a smug look.

Slade smacked him in the chest. "Ass."

"You can give the kids horsey rides." Magnus was laughing as Slade hit him again. "Teach them all about horse play."

"Quit it, Mags." Slade was going to strangle the man, if he didn't die laughing first.

Magnus gave him a look so falsely innocent Slade was surprised he wasn't struck by lightning on the spot. "What? I'm just horsing around."

Sylvia was laughing so hard she was crying.

"What about—"

Slade shut him up the best way he could think of, kissing the man until his brains leaked out of his ears. He could say one thing about his mating with Sylvia and Magnus: it would never be boring

Chapter Twelve

"Well?" Frederica lifted the teapot, almost frowning as she saw her hands were shaking with rage. She took a deep breath, trying to calm herself.

Once again Oliver had fucked things up for her. He'd interfered in her plans, going after Sylvia and Sydney, forcing them to flee their apartment. And where had the two disloyal bitches gone?

Right to Loki.

Of course.

She should have seen it coming. Something had been off that day, but she'd ignored her instincts, certain the pair were on her side. But no. Sydney, timid little rabbit that she was, had bolted to her favorite hidey-hole, Loki's home. And Sylvia had followed right behind her BFF.

Ugh. Even worse, Frederica didn't know who she was angrier with, them for running or herself for trusting them. She should have had Nadine or Sonia take care of it, but neither of them could hold a candle to Sydney Saeter when it came to hacking.

She should never have allowed Sylvia and Sydney to pair up. Sylvia was far too protective of the little rabbit. There was no way she'd allow Sydney to run to Loki alone. And now they were beyond her reach, their loyalty given to her treacherous grandchildren and the despicable Loki. She didn't care that Loki had saved her son from Odin. Odin could rot in Hel.

No. Loki had turned Baldur's mind against her, leaving her without her only child. He'd known Baldur was alive, allowed her to grieve, and for that he would *pay*.

"The new wards are far stronger than anything I've ever seen, my lady." Nadine Grimm quietly thanked Frederica as she picked up her tea cup. Here, at least, was one whose loyalty Frederica never had to question. Gná had been with her for so many centuries neither of them could count them. "I can't penetrate them."

Frederica set down the teapot before she threw it. She'd owned it since the time of Queen Victoria and was far too fond of it to shatter it in her anger. There was no discounting Nadine's words. Nadine could break into almost anything.

Almost, and that was the key. If Nadine said she couldn't penetrate the new wards and retrieve Sydney and Sylvia, it could not be done.

"However, I believe I can lure at least one of them out, but it will take a day or two to set things up."

"Do it." With luck they would capture Sydney. If not, Sylvia would do as a bargaining chip. "And the other matter?" She lifted the tea cup, praying that this matter, at least, would have a happy resolution.

"I am close to finding him, but he's being protected." Nadine sipped her tea calmly, not fearing her lady's rage in the least. Nadine knew Frederica's temper well, another reason they got along. Frederica's anger had rarely been turned on Nadine, and when it had been, Nadine had accepted her punishment gracefully. "I fear Njord may be involved. It's the only explanation that makes sense."

The cup almost slipped from Frederica's hand. "Njord?" Why would the god of the sea interfere in her hunt for Jörmungandr? Surely he would want the Serpent destroyed just as much as she did.

"It's possible he wishes the kill for himself, but I doubt it." Nadine leaned back, her gaze speculative. "I fear he may be on Kiran's side in this."

"Baldur." Frederica refused to use that name, the name of the man who'd betrayed her. To her, he would always be Baldur.

"Yes, my lady." Nadine responded gently to the rebuke and continued. "I fear Odin may be the true problem, however. The wolf, Fenris, was unable to wound him."

"I've considered asking Henry and Luther to go take care of him for me." Frederica frowned as Nadine shook her head. "And why not?"

"You will lose them, my lady."

When her hand trembled this time it was from fear. "You truly believe so?"

Nadine leaned forward, her calm demeanor cracking. Here was her friend, her advisor, not the warrior and assassin Frederica knew her to be. "Only the wolf can kill Odin."

"But we know now that Fenris can't wound him. Oliver healed everything Fenris did to him."

"There is one thing Odin has not thought of, my lady."

"Oh?"

Nadine sat back with a smug smile. "Fenrisùlfr is not the only lupine child of Loki."

Frederica froze before a similar smile crossed her face. The thought that Loki would lose his son not once, but twice, filled her with joy. Perhaps then he'd understand her grief and rage. That one of his children thought dead actually lived, only to see him die at the hands of one of his allies?

Oh, it would be sweet.

She lifted her tea cup in salute. "To the Avenger's hunt."

Nadine mimicked her with her own cup. "To the hunt."

***

"Have you seen Sydney?"

Slade glanced over at Sylvia as she came back into the condo. She was supposed to be visiting with her friend, but here she was, back after only ten or fifteen minutes.

Not that he'd been counting or anything. Magnus had chosen to take that time to distract him, and they'd just gotten to the part where pants were coming off when Sylvia returned, looking grim.

Magnus must have been just as confused as he was, because he stared at her blankly. "I thought you just went to see her?"

Sylvia shifted from foot to foot. "Toni said Syd told *her* she was coming here."

"And now you can't find her?" Slade pulled his pants up. Happy time with Magnus would have to wait. If Sydney was missing Sylvia would be devastated. "Before we start worrying let's check and make sure she's not with Kir, Logan and Jordan."

"Right." Magnus finished dressing and took hold of Sylvia's hands. "And if she's not, she can't have gotten too far."

Sylvia whimpered, and Slade wanted to smack Magnus upside the head. "Let's go look. Magnus, you check with Logan and Kir. If she's not there, check with Val. I have no clue why she'd go there, but it's worth a shot. Sylvia, you check with Morgan and Skye. If they haven't seen her, ask Fenris and Jeff. I'll go look for her with Travis and Jamie and then double-back to Toni. We'll meet back here."

Magnus nodded once and was out the door in a flash, followed by Sylvia.

Slade knocked on Travis's door, smiling when Jamie opened it. "Hey, have you seen Sydney?"

"Nope. Why?"

Well, he hadn't really expected her to be with Travis, but it had been worth a shot. "We can't find her, and Sylvia's worried."

Jamie nodded. "I'll get Travis. She has to be here somewhere."

Gods, he hoped so. His mate wouldn't rest if she wasn't, and for some reason Slade was beginning to suspect she wasn't. His instincts had kept him safe for centuries, and they were screaming at him that Sydney was in serious trouble.

"I'm going to check with Toni, see if she's returned to their condo. I'll meet you at my place."

"We'll rally the troops," Jamie bellowed over her shoulder. "Tyr, we need your glow bug ass out here!"

Once his eyes uncrossed and his hearing returned, Slade made his way to Toni's condo, only to find her standing outside her door with a scowl. "No Sydney?"

"No Sydney." Toni crossed her arms over her chest. "I should have skipped her happy ass over to your place myself."

As tight and angry as the words were Slade could see the concern in Toni's face. "This isn't your fault."

She rolled her eyes at him. "I was given one job. One. Protect Syd. And I fucked it up. So tell me again this isn't my fault."

He stared at her. "You too?"

She tilted her head, obviously confused.

"You think something happened to her."

Toni blew out a breath. "Yeah, I do. She was acting strange, excited and scared at the same time. I thought she was just happy she was going to visit Sylvia, but after she left I realized she was more scared than excited."

"And then Sylvia showed up looking for her." Slade cursed under his breath. "Come on. We're meeting at my place to figure out what to do."

Toni didn't acknowledge him, just strode toward his front door with all the determination of a woman on a mission. And it wasn't long before everyone else was in his condo and the story had been passed around.

No one had seen Sydney since she'd left her condo almost half an hour before.

"What should we do?" Sylvia looked not toward her mates, but to Kir, who was clutching the pendant at his neck. Clouds raced across his eyes, obscuring the crystal blue they normally were.

"Find her. How did she get out of the building without any of us knowing?" Kir's hand tightened on the pendant and the Godspear glowed in response, the light of it only dimmed by his grasp.

"We all have free passes through the wards." Logan grimaced as they all turned and stared at him. "What? You wanted to take them down every time we went out for pizza?"

Since Kir's unholy love of pepperoni and melted cheese was well known, not one of them seemed surprised that Logan would make certain his lover could get it. The clouds disappeared from Kir's eyes. "Fine. You're right."

"Wait." Sylvia held up her hand. "You think Syd just walked out of here?"

"Yup." Logan shrugged. "No one got in. No one who's not allowed can. So…"

"She walked out." Slade frowned, trying to figure out why Syd would do that. "Has she gotten any phone calls since she moved in?"

Toni shook her head. "Neither of us have, other than my captain checking up on me."

Travis exchanged a look with Logan. "You think the Old Man mimicked Toni's captain?"

"We haven't heard a peep out of him in weeks." Logan looked just as concerned as Travis did. "It's possible."

"That makes no sense. What does Toni's captain have to do with Syd?" Slade didn't know what the pair was thinking. "Check her email. Syd never leaves the computer, right?"

"Right." Sylvia gestured for Toni to follow her. "If they got to her it was through the computer, not the phone."

Slade shook his head at Travis and Logan. "None of this makes a damn lick of sense. Why go after Syd? Why try and make her leave the condo?"

"Leverage?" Jordan shrugged as they all stared at her. "Whoever convinced her to leave has to know we're going to try and get her back."

Logan cursed. "Remember how Odin got me out? He had Jamie."

"But…we're all here." Slade looked around. "That can't be how he got her out."

"Not all of us." Logan paled. "Jörmungandr."

Slade laughed. "Hell, no. There is no way the Old Man's got my brother." Before Logan could protest, Slade continued. "Jörmungandr is so far down, so deep, Odin couldn't find him. He's hiding in the deepest of the deeps, and he's not coming out until—"

"Until Njord tells him to."

Slade jumped as Nik DeWitt's voice sounded right in his ear. "Son of a *bitch*."

"Hey, now." Heimdall, the Guardian of the Bifrost Bridge, placed his hand on Magnus's shoulder. "Don't say that about our mother."

Magnus jumped, his expression startled. "What?"

Nik laughed, and Slade shivered as a sudden chill overcame him. "Forgetting your Eddas already?
One there was born in the bygone days,
Of the race of the gods, and great was his might;
Nine giant women, at the world's edge,
Once bore the man so might in arms.

Gjolp there bore him, Greip there bore him,
Eistla bore him, and Eyrgjafa,
Ulfrun bore him, and Angeyja,
Imth and Atla, and Jarnsaxa.
Strong was he made with the strength of the earth,
With the ice-cold sea, and the blood of swine."

Magnus pushed Nik's hand away. "We're cousins at best, and you know it."

Nik smiled mysteriously, but let it go. "Don't try and find Sydney, not yet."

"Why not?" Slade didn't relish trying to get Sylvia not to look for her best friend.

"She's safe and sound, and that's all that needs to be said. To remove her from where she us would upset a delicate balance that must be maintained until Ragnarrok is fully realized."

Val growled. "Where is she?"

Nik's eyes flashed. "Safe, I swear it." He took a deep breath. "Now, there are more important things to discuss than Sydney."

"Such as?" Kir crossed his arms over his chest and matched Nik look for look.

Slade shrank back against Magnus as the two powerful gods faced off. He could face jotun, could race against the wind and win, but to fight either the Guardian or Baldur was insanity itself.

"Shh." Magnus wrapped his arms around him, holding him close as he began to shiver. "I won't let anything happen to you."

Kir glanced their way, and his stance relaxed. "What do you want, Nik?"

Nik stepped forward. "Kye and I would like to pledge ourselves to you."

Kir looked startled. "Really? I thought you were going to remain impartial."

"And I thought Kye wanted nothing to do with war." Travis looked just as confused as Kir. "After we lost to the Aesir Kye went his own way." As the god of the sea, Kye, aka Njord, had simply disappeared beneath the waves. He'd rarely participated in the antics of the gods. One of the few times he had, he'd wound up being forced to marry Skadi.

That had ended so well Kye hadn't been heard from in decades. Not until Kir was given the Godspear did he rear his head out of the waves once more.

"He had a task to perform, as we all did." Nik shrugged. "His is just taking a little longer than I thought it would."

"And that's not cryptic at all." Slade scowled when Magnus began to laugh. "It's not funny."

"Is she hurt?" Slade saw Sylvia step beside him and held out his hand. She took it, but kept her gaze on Nik. "Is Syd injured?"

Nik nodded. "Nothing serious, but yes."

"Then we need to save her." Sylvia lifted her chin, that stubborn expression he was becoming familiar with taking over her features.

"No." Nik held up his hand. "This is not up for debate. She's safe and mostly sound, and that will have to do for now."

"Please."

It hurt to hear his lover beg. It hurt worse to see the refusal in Nik's eyes. "No. In this, you have to trust me. More is at stake than just Sydney."

With that, Val growled and stormed out of the condo, Sylvia and Toni hot on his heels.

Slade sagged in Magnus's embrace. "She's going after her."

"I know." Without another word, Slade and Magnus followed after Sylvia.

***

"I'm going hunting." Val glared at the closed door, practically vibrating with rage. "Nik can go fuck himself."

Sylvia couldn't agree more. "Slade and Magnus will be watching me too closely for me to get free."

"I'll go." Toni held up her hand. "Maybe I can slip in and out without Logan or Kir noticing." Toni looked happier than she had in weeks, as if just the thought of rescuing Syd was better than frozen M&M's.

Val shot her a strange look, but shrugged. "It's not Logan or Kir you need to be worried about."

Toni crossed her arms over her chest and stood her ground. "I'm going. This is what I do, Val."

Val threw up his hands in surrender. "All right. Let me know if you find out anything."

"Will do." Toni gestured for Sylvia to follow her. "All right. Can you think of anything that would have gotten Syd out of here?"

"A threat to either Jordan or Logan." Sylvia did as told, striding after Toni as the other woman led the way into the condo they were sharing. "She might also go if there was a threat against you or me."

Toni nodded and led the way into the room Syd had obviously claimed as her work space. Computer monitors lined one wall, two keyboards, a tablet, a laptop…it was a geek's wet dream, and fit her best friend to a T.

"All right. You take the laptop, I'll take command central. Let's see if we can figure this out." Toni settled in Syd's chair and began tapping at the keyboard.

Sylvia picked up the laptop and began searching. The first thing she checked was Syd's email, but nothing seemed out of the ordinary. Syd had gotten the usual spam emails about enlarging her non-existent penis, paying someone money to get more money, and even something in French that Syd couldn't read.

"Hey. I've got something odd."

Sylvia looked up from Syd's laptop to find Toni running a video on the third screen. Toni was leaning forward, studying the image through narrowed eyes before she paused it with a scowl. "Take a look at this."

Sylvia stood, placing the laptop back on the desk. What had captured Toni's attention so desperately?

"Okay." Toni rewound the video, and Sylvia realized she was watching the front of the condo complex. "Watch this."

She started the video, and Sylvia watched as Syd appeared, racing out the door and looking frantic. She darted across the street, or at least attempted to before she was nailed by a car.

"Oh fuck." Sylvia stared, horrified, as Syd was lifted off the ground and tossed into the back of the dark sedan. "Was that Nadine?"

"Who?" Toni seemed focused on something other than the car, her brow furrowed as she paused the video again. "Mother fucker."

"What?"

Toni took a deep breath and sat back. "Nothing. Just…a case I was working on." She tapped her fingers on the desk. "Who's Nadine?"

"Frederica Grimm's girl Friday." Sylvia bit her lip. "At least we know who has her now."

"Will Frederica harm her?"

"I don't think so. She's got a plan for her." As long as Syd was useful she'd be safe. Frederica was determined, but she wasn't demented like Odin was. "She'll lock her up, but I don't think she'll abuse her."

Toni nodded, staring at the monitor in thought. After a few moments, she finally spoke. "Then I say we let her follow through with her plan."

"Why?"

"Because I'm positive Syd will figure out a way to get in touch with us without letting her captors know. Once we have a clue what Frederica's plan is, we can rescue Syd and stop Frederica without too much trouble."

"You can't go into this thinking you'll have backup and that she'll go to jail." Sylvia tilted her head. "Well, you *will* have backup, but it will be Val, Logan, Kir and the rest of the nuthouse."

Toni grimaced. "Still, what better way to stop Frederica than to leave Syd in there? I mean, you're sure she won't be hurt, right?"

Sylvia nodded. "Frederica's a bitch, but she's not crazy. Not like Oliver."

"Good." Toni leaned back. "Then we wait for Syd to contact us. Val is out looking, so we let him do that. Frederica will get suspicious if we leave Syd without making any attempt at getting her home again, and Val is the best one to send for that. He's obvious."

"I don't think you give him enough credit. Val waited for centuries to kill Oliver, and when he had the chance he took it." He'd sliced Odin's throat, stabbed him in the back and cut the major artery that ran by Odin's groin. Odin should have perished, but the stupid prophecy protected his life. The Avenger was not the one meant to kill him, so Odin survived the lethal strikes.

"Yeah, too bad it didn't work." Toni grimaced. "I'll keep watch on this end, and if I get anything that tells me that we need to extract Syd I'll contact you. You, in the meantime, stay calm. I'll get Jamie and Jeff to give me a hand, so someone will be online at all times, monitoring." She hit a couple more keys, bringing up the inside of Frederica's office. "Look."

There was Syd, sitting at the desk, her expression both terrified and filled with concentration. She was wincing as Frederica stood behind her talking to her, but other than a bruise on her cheek she seemed all right.

That was until Frederica patted Syd's shoulder and Syd flinched, her face paling. Her gaze darted toward the camera, and Sylvia could see the desperation there. Syd wanted out, away from Frederica, and was injured worse than what was visible. "I don't like this."

"Neither do I." Toni stood. "All right. You make the call. Do we go in and take her back, or leave her there?"

"We get her back." Fuck Frederica and her plans. Sylvia needed to know her friend was safe, and it was obvious she wasn't. "But what about Nik?"

"Pfft. You let me deal with Nik and his orders." Toni strode out of the office and reached for her shoulder holster. "In the meantime, let the others know what we found out. I'll get a hold of Val and come up with an extraction plan."

"Got it." Sylvia opened the door. "Thanks, Toni."

Toni nodded but didn't respond, too busy dialing her cell phone and waving an absentminded good-bye.

Sylvia returned to her own condo, worried sick for her friend, to find Slade and Magnus curled up together on the couch. They were staring at the door, looking every bit as upset as she felt. "Hi."

Magnus was the first to reach her, but Slade wasn't far behind. "You scared the crap out of us." Slade's gravelly tone was filled with fear, his arms tightening around her to the point of pain. "You aren't leaving, right? We can't risk losing you."

Magnus kissed her forehead. "If it comes down to it I'll go looking for Syd, but you aren't going anywhere."

Sylvia slumped into their embrace, letting them take her weight, and her worries. "Frederica has her, and she's banged up. Toni hacked into the security cameras around the building and saw Syd get kidnapped. We need to get her back before someone hurts her."

Magnus cupped her cheek as Slade rubbed his chin against her hair. "If you really feel that strongly about it let me go after her. I'll get her home."

Slade shivered. "No. Send Val. Hell, send fucking Kir. You're not going either."

"Slade." Magnus grabbed them both, holding them to his chest. Slade released her just enough to keep one arm around her and place the other around Magnus, holding them as tightly as he could. All of Slade's nightmares were there in the way he held them and shook.

Odin might not have broken Slade, but he'd come damn close. It would be decades, if not longer, before Slade was healed.

"I'm not going after Syd, Val and Toni are." She felt Slade relax and prayed Syd would understand. Sylvia wasn't a fighter. She'd leave that to the ones who were.

"I'll only go with someone to back me up, like Morgan."

It was the best Slade could hope for from Magnus, who was a warrior through and through. Slade sighed, and when he lifted his head from Sylvia's his expression was resigned. "Fine. But you'll be taking me with you. I'm a trained battle steed, remember?"

"And no one could catch him, not even Odin." Sylvia rather liked the idea of Slade watching Magnus's back.

Now Magnus was the one who sighed. "If we go somewhere I need a battle steed you're the only one I'd ride." He began walking them back toward the sofa. "You have a plan?"

"Toni is going to try and figure out how to get her out of there." Sylvia allowed herself to be seated between Magnus and Slade, the two men still holding on to her as if she was going to slip away from them at any moment. "Val is also looking. I'm supposed to hold down the fort and keep an eye on Syd's emails and stuff, see if she tries to contact us."

The two men exchanged a look over her head. "Nik's not gonna like that."

Nik can bite me. "It's up to Toni whether or not she helps, not Nik."

"Nik has claimed her." Magnus stroked her hair, tugging softly on the strands. "He's going to try and stop her."

Sylvia bit her lip. She had the feeling Toni was more than a match for the Guardian. "I think she can handle herself."

"If you say so." Magnus didn't sound convinced. "But we have more important things to worry about."

"Like what?" What could be more important than Syd?

Slade tilted his head, his expression thoughtful. "What color should we paint the ceiling?"

Really, he had no business looking so surprised when the pillows went flying. But that night, when her men snuggled her close after Magnus's blood bound them together, they whispered to each other in the darkness of hopes and fears and family. She was no longer alone. Syd would be saved, Ragnarrok would end Odin's reign of terror, and Sylvia would finally have the family she'd always dreamed of. It would take time, and hard work, but already they meant more to her than anyone or anything.

They would understand it when she helped Toni hunt for Syd. After all, Syd was family.

"We will." Slade's sleepy, raspy tone was so low she thought at first she'd imagined it. "As if we ever thought you'd be able to sit back and wait while your friend was out there alone."

Sylvia blinked. "Did I say that out loud?"

Slade snickered. "Yup, you did."

"You won't do this by yourself." Magnus's voice was louder, and far more determined. "You *will* let us help."

She sighed happily. "The Three Musketeers, right?"

"Right." Slade yawned.

Magnus's response was a simple kiss. "Go to sleep, d'Artagnan. We'll slay Milady de Winter tomorrow."

"Goober." She rolled her eyes.

"Bake her cookies," Slade muttered. "That will teach her to mess with you."

She glared over her shoulder at Slade. "Three Musketeers my ass. More like the Three Stooges."

The two men looked at each other and, with identical grins, echoed, "Nyuk nyuk nyuk."

"Ugh." She hid her head under the pillow. A moment later, she peeked out and whispered, "I get to be Moe."

The only reply she got was a bone-rattling snore.

Epilogue

"Are you sure about this?"

Nik desperately wanted to roll his eyes, but Kye had been through enough recently that he didn't want the guy to think Nik was mocking him. "Yes, I'm sure. Even if Logan and Kir want to say no I'm positive Travis will say yes." And while Nik respected the hell out of Kir, it was Travis he still felt fealty toward.

Oh, well. Swearing fealty to Kir wouldn't be all that big a deal for him. He'd done it for Odin, the bitter taste of defeat still fouling everything. He could swear to Kir for the sake of Antonia.

The thought of the bright, brown-eyed homicide detective made him shiver with need. She didn't want to acknowledge the pull between them, the instant flare of attraction, but Nik was going to ensure that nothing stood in the way of his claiming her. Even Kir.

"I hoped to have Ryker with us when we arrived, but he's managed to hide even from me."

"He's safe." Nik could see Jörmungandr, who'd taken the mortal name Ryker Saeter, the instant he thought of him. The World Serpent slept in the deeps, but he'd made tentative forays onto land now that Kir held the Godspear. It was one of the reasons Kye had such a hard time finding him. When the World Serpent was on land, he was invisible to Kye's senses. "You can sense him now if you try."

The relief on Kye's face didn't surprise him. Kye's reluctance to hunt Jörmungandr, his desire to keep the

Serpent safe, and his need to swear fealty to Kir all led Nik to one inescapable conclusion: the god of the sea had the hots for a snake. He'd have to wait to claim the man, though. Nik knew Ryker Saeter wasn't quite ready to join his father. Something else needed to happen before the Serpent emerged from the deeps. "Ready?"

Kye blew out a breath and squared his shoulders. "Ready."

Nik waved his hand and the two of them appeared inside the condominium complex. He would never say it out loud, but he *loved* doing that. The look on Logan's face as he tried to figure out how Nik got through the wards was priceless every single time.

Nik smiled as Jordan opened the door to her condo. "Good evening."

Her brows rose. "Good evening?" She pushed her glasses up her nose. "What are you doing here?"

He gestured behind him toward his bags and Kye. "We're moving in."

Kye waved. "Hi, neighbor."

"Shit." Jordan shook her head. "There goes the neighborhood."

Look for these titles by Dana Marie Bell

The Gray Court
Dare to Believe
Noble Blood
Artistic Vision
The Hob
Siren's Song
Never More

Halle Pumas
The Wallflower
Sweet Dreams
Cat of a Different Color
Steel Beauty
Only In My Dreams

Halle Shifters
Bear Necessities
Cynful
Bear Naked
Figure of Speech
Indirect Lines

Heart's Desire
Shadow of the Wolf
Hecate's Own
The Wizard King
Warlock Unbound

Maggie's Grove
Blood of the Maple
Throne of Oak
Of Shadows and Ash
Song of Midnight Embers

The Nephilim
*All for You
*The Fire Within
Speak Thy Name

Poconos Pack
Finding Forgiveness
Mr. Red Riding Hoode
Sorry, Charlie

*Published by Carina Press

Dana Marie Bell Books
www.danamariebell.com

Manufactured by Amazon.ca
Bolton, ON